Fuel

Fuel

75 Prize-Winning Flash Fictions
Raising Funds
To Fight Fuel Poverty

edited by

Tania Hershman

First published in 2023 by Tania Hershman

Copyright © The Authors

The right of The Authors to be identified as the authors of this work has been asserted in accordance with the Copyright Designs and Patents Act 1988

All rights reserved. No part of this publication may be reproduced, distributed, or transmitted in any form of by any means, including photocopying, recording or any other electronic of mechanical methods, without the prior written permission of the publisher.

A CIP catalogue record of this book is available from the British Library.

ISBN 978-1-7392974-0-4

Printed and bound in Great Britain
by Ex Why Zed
exwhyzed.co.uk

Cover image by Marie Leadbetter
Cover design by Katie Jacobs

www.fuelflash.net
twitter.com/fuelFlash
instagram.com/fuelflashfictionanthology

Contents

Introduction i
How to read this book iv

15-C-47662 • *Patrick Holloway* • 1
A Choice for the Golden Age • *Matthew Castle* • 5
A Girl's Guide to Fly Fishing • *Mary-Jane Holmes* • 11
After the Armourers • *Marissa Hoffmann* • 13
Battle Hymn of the American Republic • *Jeremy Galgut* • 15
Bedlam • *Jo Withers* • 17
Blue Hills Yonder • *Joanna Will* • 18
Both On and Off • *Jack Barker-Clark* • 20
Buttercups • *Terry Warren* • 22
Cleft • *Gaynor Jones* • 24
Coffee • *Barbara Kuessner Hughes* • 26
Darling Mummy • *Zoe Barkham* • 29
Double Lives • *Kathryn Aldridge-Morris* • 31
Drought • *David Swann* • 33
Emmylou, Patron Saint of Dirt-Poor Folks • *Sharon Boyle* • 35
Fall River, August 1892 • *Sarah Hilary* • 38
Fever • *Claire Carroll* • 40
Fifth Grade • *Brianna Snow* • 43
Fly • *Rob Walton* • 44
Fly Away Home • *Helen Rye* • 45
For You, I Am • *Alison Woodhouse* • 47
Glass • *Fiona McKay* • 48
Good for Her • *D. Brody Lipton* • 51
Granny Smith, Queene • *Elisabeth Ingram Wallace* • 53
Groceries • *Tania Hershman* • 56
How Much Rain Can a Cloud Hold? • *Laurie Bolger* • 59
I Found Myself Lost • *Pauline Masurel* • 62
If A Tree Falls • *Rachel O'Cleary* • 66

In The Car • *Bernadette M Smyth* • 69
La Loba • *Vicki Jarrett* • 72
Last, Best Hope in a Shade of Orange • *Taria Karillion* • 77
Lessons in Attachment Parenting • *Sara Hills* • 81
Lost Appetite • *Bean Sawyer* • 84
Morning Routine • *Kim Catanzarite* • 85
Mouse • *Gillian O'Shaughnessy* • 87
Mum Died • *Rowena Warwick* • 89
Mum's The Word • *Valerie O'Riordan* • 91
Never Let Me Go • *Cathy Lennon* • 93
One Of The Girls • *Monica Dickson* • 94
Plum Jam • *Frances Gapper* • 98
Polio • *Nicholas Ruddock* • 99
Press 3 for Random Track • *Dri Chiu Tattersfield* • 101
Recesses • *Brenden Layte* • 106
Scrolling Facebook Memes While Waiting For The Paediatrician • *Elisabeth Ingram Wallace* • 111
Sea Change • *Sharon Telfer* • 116
Search History • *Iain Rowan* • 118
Self/Less • *Electra Rhodes* • 120
Silent Space • *Jane Roberts* • 126
Sins of the Heart • *Kit de Waal* • 128
Snow Crow • *Doug Ramspeck* • 130
Sometimes There's Compassion in a Punch • *Peter Burns* • 132
Teavarran • *Louise J Jones* • 135
Ten Months With Octopus • *Angela Readman* • 137
The Button Wife • *Dara Yen Elerath* • 142
The Cinders of 2021 • *Kevin Cheeseman* • 144
The Eight Year Hope Of Us • *Lucy Goldring* • 148
The First Man on The Moon • *Rosie Garland* • 150
The Grand Finale • *Tim Craig* • 152
The Hand That Wields the Priest • *Emily Devane* • 154
The Haunted Pan • *Phil Olsen* • 156

The Letter From The Home Office • *Gail Anderson* • 159
The Lighthouse Project • *Vanessa Gebbie* • 161
The Long Wet Grass • *Seamus Scanlon* • 164
The Most Fascinating Woman in the World • *Andrew Boulton* • 166
The Reminder • *Ida Keogh* • 169
The Shop Game • *Sam Payne* • 174
The Wall • *Mandy Wheeler* • 177
Things Left and Found by the Side of the Road • *Jo Gatford* • 181
Things the Fortune Teller Didn't Tell You When She Read Your Fortune • *Iona Rule* • 183
To Pieces • *Abby Feden* • 186
Treating the Strains and Stains of Marriage • *Sherry Morris* • 191
Twenty-one Species of Fish Called Sardine • *Rosaleen Lynch* • 194
Undergrowth • *Melissa Bowers* • 198
We Will Go On Ahead and Wait for You • *Michael Logan* • 200
While My Wife is Out of Town • *Jude Brewer* • 202

Contributor Biographies • 205
Competition Descriptions with Story Titles • 230
Index of First Lines • 244
Acknowledgements • 249

Introduction

The seed that grew into the idea for this book was planted in the summer of 2022, as I listened with distress to the news about increasing electricity, gas and petrol prices in the UK, and heard stories of people already being forced to choose between heating their food and heating their home. I wanted to do something more than just donating money to food banks, to fuel poverty charities. Putting together an anthology of flash stories—which here means short short stories under 1500 words or so, sometimes *much* shorter—I could do easily, I thought. I have all the contacts, and the flash fiction community is such a generous one, I felt sure people would be happy to be involved.

Then I had another thought: what if I did something that hadn't been done before? What if this was not just a fundraising book that people would buy to help a cause but a book that both celebrates dozens of brilliant flash stories that had won first prize in competitions around the world and, at the same time, explodes the myth that there is any kind of "formula" for a winning story by showcasing 75 examples of what a winning story *might* be?

As I had hoped, the flash community—both the competition organisers and the authors of the winning stories—were incredibly generous in helping me and donating their stories. And, even if I say so myself, I do think the book you hold in your hands is fantastic. Here are 75 flash fictions that have all won first prize in a competition—the earliest from 2006, the newest just last year—and look at the range of lengths, styles, forms, voices, genres! Look at the myriad different ways to tell stories to appeal to all manner of readers, from the more linear and "conventional" stories to the experimental, the minimalist, the all-one-sentence-with-no-full-stops story, the bullet point story, the story as play, as email chain, as letter.

At a certain point, and with some reluctance, I decided to include one of my own winning flash stories; I realised as I was compiling the anthology that a number of the stories put forward by competition organisers were ones that I myself had picked as the winner when I had the honour of judging their competitions. This would be a good chance, I thought, to explode *another* myth: that a judge must be drawn to the kind of stories they write themselves. Take a look, if you'd like, at my story, *Groceries* (p56) and then have a read of the stories I chose as winners of various competitions (*Good For Her* (p51); *Granny Smith, Queene* (p52); *Morning Routine* (p85); *Mum's the Word* (p91); *One of the Girls* (p94); *Sins of the Heart* (p128); *While My Wife is Out Of Town* (p202)), and see what you think.

I hope that you will find this book both entertaining and useful, that it will introduce you to new favourite writers and to competitions to send your own work to if you yourself are a writer. Most of all, I hope that the astonishing range of stories here will give you permission to write the story you want to write in the way you want to write it, however long or short that story needs to be.

Thank you so much for buying this anthology and helping support fuel poverty charities—may our book outlive the need for the assistance these charities offer to those who are struggling.

Happy reading!

Tania Hershman
Manchester, UK
February 2023

How To Read This Book

There are many ways to enjoy a book of very short flash fictions by many authors, which are presented here in alphabetical order by title. You might cast your eye down the contents page and see which title demands that you read it! (As a competition judge, titles are very important.) You might leaf through and read stories at random. You might look for the shortest stories first. Or the longest.

If you'd like to read all the stories that have won a particular competition, you can turn to the Competition Descriptions section at the back of the book (p230), where you will find a list below each competition's bio.

Another thing that will grab a judge's attention is the first line of a story, so I thought I'd include something that's often seen in poetry anthologies: an Index of First Lines (p244). Head over there and see which one whets your appetite—and take a moment to marvel over all the many ways to begin a story!

15-C-47662
Patrick Holloway
Winner, Flash 500 Flash Fiction Competition, Q3 2021

1.

Your teeth are smudged blueberry. You hold one in between finger and thumb, examining it as if it were a world. You are the same age as me but I feel like you have been here before. Your foot flirts with my leg under the table. It is hard to be so alive sometimes, trying to take in too much. You say something and I miss it, lost to unformed futures. Your leg pulls away. You drop the blueberry to the ground and sigh— I can see the air and something else leave your exaggerated mouth, something earthy.

2.

In the moments after, your fingers are too soft, tracing veins up and down my arm. There is a rare silence to you and I think you are happy. The thought alone speeds everything up while slowing everything down. There are a hundred of you and only now do they move in unison, kicking two hundred perfect feet free from the blanket. All those mouths echoing, so much breath against my neck.

3.
Your teeth grind, feet tapping the concrete as your arms swing by your side. Pupils the size of blueberries. The music flees from the club and whatever we left is something already altogether different. You hold the wall and vomit splatters against your bare legs. I look down and there are so many shadows fighting for space on the grey stage of memory.

4.
You bite my lip too hard and draw blood. You spit it out and say sorry and shrug as if you are not sorry. You crumple up like a sweet wrapper. Folded into yourself, you cry, then scream when I try to get closer. A few crimson drops drip from me as I lean down and stain the carpet floor.

5.
I call you. Drive to the apartment you rent. Call your mum. The day is enveloped in the night and opens out above me. You are gone and I tell everyone you will be back. Inside of me there are only chambers I cannot come out from. Each one a morsel of time with you.

6.
A year passes.

7.
Fifteen more.

8.
When they find your car it is because a part of the registration is still visible at the bottom of the tide; a sepulture of silt. The smell of the car comes back to me, not the colour, or anything else, just the smell of pine that used to remind me of Curraghbinny woods, and how frightened I'd be on school trips there, or looking out at the trees under the moon, knowing people were hanged there back in the war. We walked there once and I watched how your head bent so far back to take in the sheer height of the oak, the birch, the ash.

9.
They find no remains for the first few days. I do not talk about it much but people text me, people I haven't spoken to in so long. My son and daughter ask me what is wrong and I say I am just tired, which is the best truth of a lie I can muster. Inside of me acute edges try to fit themselves into something the shape of your eyes. At night I cannot look at my wife.

10.
A tooth. A molar. A broad surface for grinding. For breaking things down. That doesn't break down. I think it must be the one from the top right of your mouth, the only one that didn't have ugly, copper fillings.

11.
All that time down there in the depths of yourself.

12.
You were gone longer than I knew you.

13.
I see you smile now, moving like a silk scarf falling from the pier. I see it ripple the surface, imbibing all the air and salt and softly drowning, beautifully.

A Choice for the Golden Age

Matthew Castle, winner, 2017 Shoreline of Infinity Flash Fiction Competition

The Captain wakes, reborn into the Golden Age for the sixteenth time.

"Welcome back, sister," says Ship. "We're nearly there."

Aiko's eyes snap into focus. She recognises Ship's voice, her immediate surroundings, and the same old sequence of sensation and thought that has followed each of her embodiments to date. The unnerving sharpness in the lines and corners of the printing chamber's ceiling, the tickle of an air current on her cheek, and the never-answered question that bursts into her mind each time: I am awake, but am I alive?

Even as she flexes each new finger and waggles each new toe, she explores her wider sensorium, evaluating the status of the Golden Age: the ship, the crew, the sleepers, and the progress of the journey.

She swings her legs off the fabrication table and takes two cautious steps towards the mirrored hatch. She looks herself up and down, and giggles: she is a child.

Short, shiny-skinned, narrow-jointed and unmistakably non-biological, but elegant nonetheless. She estimates her mass to be around eighteen percent less than the last time she was embodied, which was—as she forms the question, Ship soundlessly supplies the answer—eight hundred and sixty three years ago. She's smaller and a little less human each time she wakes.

"Guess we're really pushing against matter-energy constraints now," she says aloud, testing the sound of her voice. It is a simple electronic speaker system this time, and the tone is high and piping. She giggles again, like tinkling water. She was always a good talker. She'll never need to stop for breath again.

"We've had to consume significant reaction mass in course adjustments," says Ship. "And most systems are approaching their resilience thresholds. We've had a number of closed loop failures. Non-linearities are proliferating. And there's a choice to be made. That's why the voyagers wanted you back, rather than the rostered primary crewmember. The Golden Age needs its captain."

Aiko nods. She reaches for the hatch, but stops suddenly, and gasps.

"What is it, Aiko?" asks Ship.

"A dream. I was dreaming."

There are several types of sleeper on the Golden Age. At any one time there are two or three active human crew. Their primary role, other than maintaining biological continuity, is to manage the ship's zoo and gardens. They grow and eat food, make love, raise children, and sleep and dream in the age-old way.

And there are the cold sleepers, the two hundred-odd descendants or surrogated offspring of the original crew, whose metabolism has been slowed to a crawl by cryoprotectants and ever-more tenuously preserved hibernation technology. A complex Ship-devised algorithm rotates them out of cold sleep at an optimal premenopausal moment, and suggests when to rotate their adolescent children back into hibernation, taking numerous parameters—including physical and personal developmental milestones and ship resource constraints—into some unknowable account. Cold sleepers dream, but never remember.

Then there are many thousands of gametes, frozen boilerplate embryos, and whole-person encodable genome sequences. Less than thirty percent of the embryos remain viable after a dozen millennia, but that still leaves a veritable treasure trove of human diversity. It is the sleep of possibility; a dreamless resting potential.

Finally, there are the uploaded: the preserved mind states of former crew. Ship's network storage substrate is a finite resource, and a human mind takes up a lot of space, so not everyone gets uploaded. The Golden Age's original crew are permitted this privilege, as they form a vital first-hand link with the terrestrial culture that built and launched the Golden Age. Usually, at least one avatar-embodied mind state is active at any one time, passing knowledge and traditions to the newer generations. Between embodiments, the uploaded crew consume few resources, evolving at a glacial pace: the minimum required for self-coherence.

Ship's avatar meets Aiko outside the printing chamber.

"We'll go straight to the viewing gantry," Ship says. "You can tell me about your dream on the way."

Ship is a smooth, metallic skinned human-sized figure motionless in repose, but implacable in motion. Aiko glides smoothly, despite her toy-like appearance.

"I've never dreamed in upload before." The metal floors are worn and the walls are thinner than Aiko remembers; the Golden Age is consuming herself as she nears the end of her voyage. "There's a door at the end of a curving wooden walkway. Water laps underneath." She tries to slow down, but her little legs appear to be slaved to Ship's long, relentless stride. "There are plants in the windows. Someone is waiting."

They emerge onto the viewing gantry, and join a small family.

There's a man. He wears hooded coveralls with soil-stains on the knees and elbows. There's a woman, and a boy. Two males: earlier generations of crew would have regarded this as wastefully suboptimal. She reviews their life histories again: they're good people. But they seem nervous, today.

"We're honoured by your embodiment, Grandmother-Captain," says the woman. She looks confused; perhaps wondering why Ship made Aiko so small.

"We are at an important point in our journey," Aiko says, "and a decision needs to be made."

Aiko gazes out. A globe fills the screen. It's a representation of a terrestrial planet situated in the habitable zone of the K class star Groombridge 1618: their destination.

In most respects, Ship is the real master of the Golden Age, of course. But for now, there is still a former human in the loop.

It's a simple binary decision. Decelerating will consume over half the mass of the Golden Age. If human biological continuity is to be maintained, all that clunky, hopelessly outdated wetware and its associated supporting paraphernalia—the cold sleepers, the gametes, the embryos and the crispvats—must be preserved. Weighed against that is a future refined and optimised over many centuries of travel: the processing substrate that hosts Ship's Mind, and the minds of all Aiko's old crewmates.

The Captain remembers the rest of her dream, and chooses.

A Girl's Guide to Fly Fishing
Mary-Jane Holmes, winner, Reflex Flash Fiction Competition, Autumn 2019

It wasn't the fly fisher's fault she got caught up in his line, she was too busy rootling in her handbag for a hanky to be paying attention. She felt the hook at her hairline, the lift of skin at the base of her occiput as she catapulted towards the lake. The water was a shock, cold, murk-green, but as soon as she was submerged, she was in the air again, widgeons scattering, lapwings barrel-rolling. The sensation was akin to how the stomach cadenzas when driving a bump in the road at 70 miles an hour or one of those tight orgasms you feel in the small of the back when you've just met someone, something she'd almost forgotten about.

After a while, the fly fisher reeled her in. "We're not doing it right," he said.

"You sound like my husband," she said, picking minnows out of her teeth.

"It's not you, I was fishing salmon, but this might be trout territory."

She wringed out her hair; he pulled out a box full of feathers, furs and beads.

His fingers were soft against her skin as he wove the fluff of marabou across her scalp, wrapped black chenille round the wire, tied off the hackle with gemstones until she was the perfect bait.

The fly fisher's touch was as light as a water skeeter, she was as iridescent as a damselfly, but still no catch rose to the surface and then just as he was going to reel her in for the last time, there it was: a prism of scales, mouth a wide O gunning towards her. She grabbed it by the gills, kissed its puckering lips, felt the fizz of oxygen between them, the lift of the rod back onto dry land.

After the Armourers

Marissa Hoffmann, winner, 2021 Mslexia Flash Fiction Competition

For what Giorgi did, the clansmen could have thrown wood tar on him, rolled him in feathers, hanged him. But that isn't their way.

They load him with vodka. He doesn't fight them. They shave his head and push him shirtless in a wheelbarrow into the square, digging a path in the snow.

Beneath the ancient tree, the men position Giorgi on a stool in the low sun, the blessed noose above him.

Some of the men smoke while they watch their wives choose. The women are used to being watched, even by each other. They take either a fist size rock from a knee-high pile, or a dinner spoon from a neatly arranged row on a trestle table erected especially for the purpose.

And afterwards, Giorgi is weak.

The women leave, and then the church clock fidgets over the children who are made to queue before him—Georgi's own among them—little Aleksander, tear-smudged, and Magda, her hair, sleeping-deep-oil black, veiling her face. At least she knows he tried to help her escape the marriage.

Giorgi thinks of the secret twelfth birthday party for Magda where her friends swung from his biceps.

One by one, the children warm their spoon in a haaaa of breath. They hang it against Giorgi's cold bare back and chest. The taller children build a collar around his shoulders. The smaller ones make a twinkling bib over Giorgi's belly.

Giorgi is still. If a single spoon drops from his skin, the men will begin to throw the rocks. They have no choice.

Magda places her spoon over her father's heart. Aleksander, smiling at the game now—knowing where the spoon sticks best—stretches, he tiptoes towards his father's nose. Giorgi smiles and helps his little man reach; he bows.

Battle Hymn of the American Republic
Jeremy Galgut, winner, 2012 Writers & Artists Flash Challenge

Julia Ward Howe in her room on the second floor of the Willard Hotel gathers the sheets around her. She sings softly, cupping her pale hands around her mouth in case the sleep of the man next door is disturbed.

When she heard the song at the parade and her companion suggested she re-write it—"something deeper, my dear, less of the doggerel and more like an anthem"—her blood grew warm and the words began to form immediately.

There is a phrase she must check in the bible: "A terrible swift sword." She breathes in. Her unconscious belongs to the gospel tellers and the red-faced priest of her childhood who was as solid as the mountain and possessed of a certainty now beginning to crumble everywhere.

She gets up and takes out her writing paper, for it is time to record her creation before it seeps away. She walks across the room to find her blouse. Almost shamefully she scribbled phrases on the cuffs as they came to her, out of sight of the companion.

That soldier who sang "John Brown" at the parade had such a rich voice...the night is calm, but she can hear the music, louder now, thunderous. Her pen is quick and still she sings, raising a palm in apology to the man next door who may be turning distractedly in his sleep. She cannot stop for anything.

When the first draft is finished she goes to the window. Julia Ward Howe is intoxicated, full of the world outside this room of drying petticoats and stale flowers. She closes her eyes and puts her ear to the glass to hear the sound of battlefields and churches and the soldier in the distance singing her new words.

Bedlam

Jo Withers, winner, 2019 Flashback Fiction Moon Microfiction Competition

I sit rigid, body taut as wooden chair. Physicians unleash freezing water against flesh, hoping to exorcise hysteria.

They blame the moon, say its phases corrupt menstrual cycles. Tighten restraints during waxing and waning, confine us to horsehair padded cells when radiance is full. They call us Luna-tics, smell delirium in the disobedience of husbands, in childbirth and menopause, frigidity and sexuality, in grief over lost children.

We never go outside. The moon is an oil lamp overhead, night and day, on and off. Eventually we forget sky and birds and trees. Eventually we become everything they said we were.

Blue Hills Yonder
Joanna Will, winner, 2020 Mslexia Flash Fiction Competition

Is hard to bind heart to harrow and drill. I am ever becoming silver wind in aspen, indigo swallow tracing curve of brook.

Is harder still to enter farmhouse with dead shadowless corners, with magic dropping from shoulders like cloak.

I turnover plow in Bottom Gully and Papa he mishappy. He hold up poor fingerless hand and say, This is what happened to me, Boy, to stop my dreaming.

Oh but I cannot halt dreaming of Blue Hills Yonder across wide vale. And they drawing light of my eye from furrow and stook. They lying in ranges of colour from dark to cornflower to sky, curving gentle like woman resting on side in meadow.

I say, Why McKellan hills so Blue?

And Papa he say, They are green like any other.

He look at me some.

Son. The morrow you go to McKellan's farm. Take my purse for a chestnut filly.

I walk wide vale the livelong day. I come to McKellan yonder and give him Papa's gold.

With bright filly I cross the hillside, deep grass cool like living water. Filly feed on freshest slope of green, and I see my Papa's words was true.

I spy over vale to our own home hills—and they the very Blue of Heaven! Oh, my aspen and brook, my swallows, land where our name rest on gravestones. My own place of root is Blue Hills Yonder!

And Angel of Peace, she stretch soft wing of feather about my heart.

Both On and Off
Jack Barker-Clark, winner, 2021 Fish Flash Fiction Prize

On the phone to your daughter all winter. On the power of attorney. On cloud cuckoo land. On the canal boat you once owned. On bravery. On ignominy. On trial. On fresh grapes. On the occasion of your birthday. On call if you need us. On amplification. On overreaction. On hold with the doctors. On display for one month only. On our best case scenario. Onwards and upwards. On lovely shiny wet new grapes.

On modern medicine. On the contrary. On the one hand not so bad. On the other hand terminal. On assisted living. On your head be it. On the bedside table, there, next to your reading glasses. On increasing medication. On a tour of hospitals, West Yorkshire, the surrounding Humber. On the formal bed, writing down what the doctor had said. On *dyschronometria* and *cerebellar lesions*. On lovely shiny wet new grapes.

On the ward. On the pillows inmates rest on. On-demand westerns. On John Wayne. On horseback. On purpose. On the bathroom floor with the shower gel. On the bathroom floor with the shower gel following a stroke. On disturbing volcanic dreams now. On canal boats choked with weeds. On holiday in 1972. On ghost trains. On beach towels. On lovely shiny wet new grapes.

On average twenty beats per minute. On life support. On your own. On top of the breadbin. On all sides surrounded. On the way. On the beach with Eleanor. On the borderlands. On the grass slopes. On and on. On Wednesday the 20th March. On and on, and then suddenly off.

On behalf of those who knew him. On behalf of those who knew him best. On behalf of his grandson, unable to attend. On the TransPennine Express writing letters to his grandad who had died.

Buttercups

Terry Warren, winner, 2017 Bridport Flash Fiction Prize

People come.

People say: "I expect you expect her to come walking right through that door any minute."

People do actually say that.

"What door might that be?" I might say, "The bathroom door? The attic door? The louvre bi-fold door to the airing cupboard?"

I might say that. But mostly I just shake my head and tell them not at all, I can face the facts, I know the reality. I know you won't be texting or e-mailing either. After all I got her ashes here on the Welsh dresser, ain't I? Next to the medicine.

Of course, there's scientists that say a) "A particle can exist in two or more states of being simultaneously" and that there are tons of other alternative universes where It never happened and everything's okay. That's scientific fact.

Or they say with absolute and complete certainty that b) We are all just part of some simulated, virtual world. So you and me, the children, the dogs, the cat—

we've never really existed. All of which seems like a total bloody waste of time to me.

I have my own ideas.

c) You're just hiding.

The cat clawed me in the night; I was sleeping on your side of the bed.

I picked you buttercups from the meadow this morning.

Huge armfuls; my shirt turned yellow. They don't last long.

The people have gone.

You can come out now.

Any door you like.

Cleft

Gaynor Jones, winner, Bath Flash Fiction Award, June 2019

noun
    a fissure or split
    indentation in the middle of a person's chin
    a deep division

Cleft. As belonging to me, my father, his father before him, their fathers before them. Runs way back in our men, as my father used to tell me while he shaved.

Boy, you could find this cleft of ours nuzzled next to the stock of a Henry rifle, or buried deep between the long legs of a good time girl in an old time saloon. You'll see.

My father was proud. That dent in his skull meant something to him, though he had no hand in its making. Soon as I was old enough to shave myself—and all that came with it—he would come for me. Head tilted up. Chin jutting out.

    Him: Eyes like tar and a hand rubbing the indent at the bottom of his drawn face.

    Me: In for some shit.

He would grab me, in that convenient little nook that perfectly fit his thumb and forefinger. Force me towards whatever he needed me to see.

Exhibit A: magazines he'd found under my mattress.

Exhibit B: a journal entry I hadn't torn up enough before burying in the trash.

Exhibits C through Z: scripture.

Then: Firm hands gripping my chin, strong arms turning me.

Now: Loose flesh, weak arms, still trying to turn me.

"What you two do in your bedroom is one thing, boy, but to bring a child into that. *A child.*"

My son's face is perfect. Moon-round. I bounce him on my knee, or pat him after his milk and he looks up at me and I look down at him and it is love. While we play, his small hands reach up to my chin, and vanish in the hairs of my beard.

Coffee

Barbara Kuessner Hughes, winner, Flash 500 Competition, Q3 2018

Margaret drinks coffee rarely; it's too emotive. She doesn't always want to return to Malaya in 1952. But today she's weary.

She turns her teaspoon, thinking of other brown waters.

The sluggish ochre flow of a rainforest river. A gibbon whoops in an emerald tree above the boat. The outboard motor coughs. Sitting on Father's lap, Margaret fingers the craters of his bullet scars. His shirt is as damp as the humid air, his thin face lathed leaner by former torments.

Their home, the plantation manager's house by the river, is raised on pillars to exclude snakes and floodwaters. The corrugated-iron roof deafens when thundering rains crash. There is papaya for breakfast, curry for dinner.

Margaret enjoys following Father when he talks to the Tamil tappers. He smiles and jokes, unlike at home. She runs along solemn rows of grey-barked trees with diagonal cuts in their trunks, and cups to gather the sap.

A birthday party for three, cake with coffee icing.

Disgruntled with prettiness wasted, sociability stifled, Mother changes the record to Sinatra and slits her eyes disdainfully. The smoke from mosquito coils rises toward the sunset sky.

Rubber estates are oppressive, Mother says, the life lonely and dull.

Father frowns. It's a living. Bloody Hollywood fantasies! If you're bored, read! Just be happy! Didn't the War teach you anything? Or the Japanese? It's an Emergency! The Communists could shoot us dead tomorrow.

They sit in a coffee shop in town. Margaret tastes condensed milk and coffee, sweet and heavy in her mouth. There's a Chinese calendar with slashing scarlet calligraphy. A red roasted duck hangs up by its neck. She stares at a fly buzzing around the table as jagged words collide above her head.

Back in the now, Margaret pours more milk into her coffee to weaken its impact.

White slips and panties are spread out on her parents' bed. An empty suitcase awaits.

A few days later, a void opens and engulfs the whole house. Father drinks many dark and golden liquids. Never coffee.

She gazes at the white café tablecloth.

The letter comes in a white envelope, addressed to her, yet writing past and over her. No explanation that she has ever accepted, even now.

Father is withdrawn in the evenings, finally vanquished. His white shirt looms in the dusk as she looks out onto the veranda and tries to enliven him with her thoughts.

She seeks comfort in the kitchen, in the arms of Malay servants who murmur to her and pity her, and sometimes love her.

Time and the river flow ponderously past. Father sends her to a convent school. He doesn't concern himself with details.

Another piece of paper, a ticket, eventually bears her away to another life. A better life than she anticipated.

She looks up, wondering why she ever drinks coffee, why she doesn't try harder to evade these associations. She sees the father of her children, smiling at her as he strides through the door of the cafe.

Darling Mummy

Zoe Barkham, winner, 2010 Fish Flash Fiction Prize

Darling mummy,

Well, the big day is here at last! I do so wish you and Daddy could be here, but it's a terribly long drive down from Yorkshire and it'll all be over so quickly that it hardly seems worth the trip. So you're not to fret, and besides, Bobby is here. She popped in last night, and she's promised faithfully to tell you everything just as soon as she gets back.

Anyway, everything is ready. I feel very calm, which is nice, because when I married Archie I was in a fearful flap, wasn't I? Oh, mummy, I know you and Daddy wanted me to stay married to Archie for ever, but really, I couldn't. Anyway, Archie's dead now, and there's nothing to be done about it. I'm sorry I couldn't get to the funeral, though I do see it would have been rather odd-looking, but Bobby said it all went off splendidly. I hear they had "The Son of God Goes Forth to War," which I think is bad taste given that the poor old chap took it between the eyes from his service revolver.

The vicar's been trying to get me into a suitable frame of mind for this morning, even talking about Archie and saying I'll see him in Heaven. In that case, I hope I'm going the other way (sorry, mummy) because it was bad enough being Mrs Archie on earth, let alone for all eternity.

Gosh! There's the bell. Now, mummy, you're not to worry about me, because I'm not a bit nervous. You know I've always been brave – remember the time I fell off Pippin? I didn't squeak then, even when they set my arm. It didn't hurt a bit. And I don't suppose being hanged will, either.

All my love,
Belinda

Double Lives
Kathryn Aldridge-Morris, winner, 2022 QuietManDave Flash Fiction Prize

I see Gwen at the school gates and she does this thing where she's looking but not seeing and I'm not in the mood so I wave my hands in her face and she says sorry, but she's still got this unseeing expression and I ask is everything ok? and she says yeah, if finding out your husband's living with another woman in the arse end of Wales is ok, and I say what, you mean your husband Rhys? and she nods, and says yes, my husband Rhys, and it's a crazy way for us to be carrying on because she only has one husband, but I'm not getting it, so I say Rhys Rhys? and she says, Rhys Rhys, and I feel a kind of vertigo because it was only last March when I noticed how he'd started hanging back after dropping the kids off, how easy it was to talk to him about all the stuff no one else ever wants to talk about, like how we all create our own prisons and how we'll bring our kids up to know there are more choices out there, how I was the only mother he spoke to, the only mother whose jokes he laughed at, and how good it felt to crack a crooked smile in the face Gwen always described as being like a slapped backside—and I think they've been together since they were fifteen, to be honest, I had thought a lot about that, about getting to your forties and only sleeping with one other person and if Rhys had ever thought about sleeping with other women before—before that first crazy time—and Gwen says she's going to get a test from the pharmacy because how many other women has he been sleeping with, and I'm like, you think there could have been *more?* and she shrugs, and I'm getting this weird double vision thing where the canopies on the horse chestnuts in front of us aren't lined up with the trunks and my left arm starts going numb, and I say, I'm not feeling too good and she says, Rhys told me you got migraines, and says, bye then, so I say, bye then, and watch her go; double-Gwen surrounded by an aura of fucked electrical impulses only I can see.

Drought
David Swann, winner, 2016 Bridport Flash Fiction Prize

In hills north of the famous resort, we slip stiles beyond the dam, looking for signs.

The tourists must be thirsty in their boarding-houses. They've left black lines around the valley's basin. The reservoir is dwindling, its mud cracked.

Miles away, they'll be rinsing sand from their kids' feet, comparing the heat to Spain. But here, save for the fruit-machine twitter of sparrows, it's quiet. A breeze off the moors. Ghosts in the wires.

My mother and I pause on a fallen wall under the shadow of a tree, watching wading-birds, busy as librarians in their aisles. Ahead is an island that's maybe the hill my grandfather sledged as a child.

She isn't sure. So much has changed since they evacuated the villagers and flooded their valley. An old tale: the few make way for the many. Only the bridge gained pardon. She points out its arch, a whale rising—before turning away to study a tree loaded with damsons.

Then she says it, with a child's wonder: "I see it now. This is my Grandma's garden."

There are sunken places, so the tales say—from which the dead call, and bells churn in storms. But the planners were cunning here, left no spires piercing the lake, only a few flattened barns and these straggling walls.

We sit on as the fruit darkens over our heads, and the shadows creep out.

They're stretched now, and thin. We watch them go down where they must, from the ruins to the water.

Emmylou, Patron Saint of Dirt-Poor Folks
Sharon Boyle, winner, Retreat West flash competition, Sept 2019

The bank sits a half mile out, as if it doesn't want anything to do with the rock-bottom town it serves. Emmylou is the only customer.

"I am robbing this bank," she says. She is pointing a gun to prove it.

The bank teller sheeshes. "First railroads, now women raiders."

"I am progress, old timer. Quit yammering, get filling." She throws him a bag.

"The swing of a rope don't scare ya, miss?"

"Hunger scares me."

The teller grins, showing baccy-blackened teeth. "You know you're goin' to hell?"

Memories flash: her ma working till sick; brothers and sisters dead; the small hands she held as the owners started their celestial journeys. The teller is right, she is going the other way.

She nods to the window. "Is that town of goddamn dullness as desperate as it looks?"

The teller cackles. "Sure is."

It's true. The minister on the other side of town is praying that progress will come—he doesn't use words like goddamn though. He wipes his neck, the air warm like the breath of a grizzly bear, and studies the funeral party before him, wondering again how he ended up among these woeful folks.

A sudden wind shakes the church.

Emmylou and the teller glance up at the bank's rafters shaken by that very same gust, before Emmylou grabs the half-filled bag and bolts. The teller waits till she crosses the threshold and lifts his gun from under the counter. The bullet gets her in the leg.

Emmylou's mouth spits curses. She hears the teller rip-skitter toward her and twists round, pistol up. One shot zips out. She doesn't know who is hit till she crumples to the ground. Her other leg. Groaning, she drops the bag. It splits open like a crooked grin.

"I ain't going to hell yet," she wheezes.

"Good," cackles the teller, "cos, I can't get frisky with a dead woman, can I?"

He pauses to ponder the notion that perhaps he can—a dearth of affection makes a man hee-haw crazy. Pondering over, he steps toward Emmylou just as the wind whorls up dollar notes in front of his face. A playful wind. He intends to be playful too.

He undoes his britches, then stops. Indignation dents his face. A crimson circle spreads on his chest. Smoke wisps from Emmylou's gun. His lips part.

"Goddamn."

The congregation leaves church: hearts heavy, stomachs light.

A flit. A flap. A burring of wings.

Folks look up, wide-eyed, at the flock of green-tinged angels swooping above.

The minister knows they have flown from the bank and if he hadn't been taught not to question he would wonder how. Instead, he blesses the soul responsible. A saint, surely.

Two souls, a half mile out, are caught on the wind. One is sucked down, *way* down. The other is buffeted upwards, as if tugged along by small hands.

Fall River, August 1892

Sarah Hilary, winner, 2008 Fish Criminally Short Histories Competition

It was such a very hot day, the air flapping like a thick cloth in her face. She escaped the chores in the house, wandered into the yard.

The prosecution said she didn't visit the barn, the dust hadn't been disturbed they said, but Lizzie remembered the baking heat of the place, so parched a stray spark might've set it alight. The whole day was like that, tinder-dry, ready to go up.

Abby was feather-dusting the furniture, fat slapping above her elbows, sweat wetting the armpits of her dress. Bridget was washing windows; you could hear the sloppy sound of the water from the back end of the yard.

The sky was stretched like the skin on a drum, the sun beating there in a fury. Lizzie turned a fretful circle in the yard. She longed for lightning to slice the sky wide open, for the kiss of rain on her sun-battered skin. She went indoors before Father returned from work. She wore the cotton calico, sky-blue. Later, she put on heavy silk, winter bengaline they called it, navy-blue with pale flowers printed on the skirt. Too much dress for such a warm day. She was glad when the police took it away.

Abby saw her coming, tried to run. Whack, whack, whack. Her head wouldn't leave her shoulders, not quite, too many rubbery rolls of flesh in the way.

Father was weary, propping his cheek on a cushion like a little boy. One whack and he was gone. Red pearls beaded the wall behind his head.

Lizzie rolled paper and lit the stove. The hot day sucked up the smoke and turned the wood to white. She thrust the axe in. Ash leapt and clung to the ruddy head of the blade, flying up from the hearth like feathers.

Fever

Claire Carroll, winner, Writers' HQ Flash Fiction Competition, Autumn 2019

Here in the dark you could be any age. Four months old and wriggling; ignorant of the difference between night and day. Three and a half in a power cut and scared of the dark. Eight with a stomach bug, whimpering in the too-big t-shirt that I put you in while I washed your pyjamas. Tonight, you are bigger than all of those earlier selves; swimming on a dark ocean. Your duvet is a fat, tired animal that crawls back over you—duller, heavier—each time you kick it away. Your legs twitch with too many hormones, too much sugar, too much blue light before bed. I stroke your hair and mutter a rosary of promises to never again allow you these things. You writhe like you're withdrawing from heroin. I google "*withdrawal heroin*". I google "*withdrawal Coca-Cola*". I google "*effects of caffeine in teens*". I google "*teen deaths from common colds*". I remember reading somewhere that a blue light can ward off sleep even if you're not looking at it. So, I turn off my phone and sit in the dark and listen to the breaking wave of each breath. Your bed is too narrow, and my body cramps around yours in a question mark. I remember lying next to you like this when you were a baby, scratching out each angry minute until I heard his key in the door.

He was always downstairs, miles out and drifting further still. Your novice immune system brought a host of plagues to my house long after he had faded to a dot on the horizon. This one wipes its nose on the soft furnishings; pesters and jostles you, pushes its way out of your mouth on the backs of insults that shatter in the air between us. Fragments glint at me now through the dark: it's my fault he's gone; you wish I had left instead; you wish he had taken you with him. I swallowed the swarm of retorts that whirred under my tongue. Instead, I dug my fingernails into the flesh of my palms, where they carved out sarcastic purple smiles. Later, I came up to find you prone and keening. You let me lie down next to you then; asked me to stroke your hair.

The grey-white of dawn seeps in past the edges of the curtains now. A hush of raindrops against the window mixes with the ebbing snarl coming from your lungs. I unfurl and ooze out of the room. You shrink with each step backwards: eight, then three, then nine months old. I float downstairs and stand—very still—in the living room. The wet morning sharpens into focus. I think how easy it would be to put my shoes on and slip out of the back door.

Fifth Grade

Brianna Snow, winner, 2017 National Flash Fiction Day Microfiction Competition

We learn that there are tubes inside of us with sleeping babies. One day, boys will wake them up. The babies will grow, open our bodies, and fall out. Until then, we'll bleed—a baby's death each month. Ms. Miller sits at her desk in the back of the room while the video plays. We turn to her to see if this is true. She's holding her stomach with both hands. We look down and do the same.

Fly

Rob Walton, Winner, 2015 National Flash Fiction Day Microfiction Competition

I'm rushing to push my lunch box into my bag when I see these two who must be flying a kite on the green triangle outside the school because she's holding a length of string, showing him how to thread it through his fingers, but then I realise she's teaching fly fishing with no river for miles and the nearest polluted anyway and I look again, and she's reading him Ted Hughes and he's hanging on every word as he casts better than anyone I've ever seen, and we all realise that rivers are just a bonus extra.

Fly Away Home

Helen Rye, winner, Reflex Flash Fiction Competition, Summer 2017

Ignition—3, 2, 1. We have a lift-off.

We have fuelled weight 28.8 tonnes. There are two hundred seconds till we escape Earth's pull and there is a ladybird on my sleeve.

S-IVB is safe. Close the PRIMARY BACK PRESSURE valve.

Ahead are the white, nuclear furnaces of stars. I have notebooks full of their speculative mechanisms and the study of matters affecting the trajectory of their satellites. I would give my flight badge for a sample the size of a rivet from one of them. And now here is a ladybird and I am four years old; my mother's hair smells of lilacs.

Pitch is tracking. Looking good.

This spacecraft weighs less than a yearling blue whale; I am blasting away from the green, swelling belly of Earth,

I can no longer see how she ripples in the wind where she has cast off the white shroud of winter and here, here is a ladybird.

GLYCOL EVAP OUTLET temperature down around 58.

Gravity is not your friend—the thing that keeps you earthbound, tied to rock and dust and this coraline sunset you see here this ocean that aquamarines the bright planet it is not a gift and all my life I have worked to escape it. And ahead, ahead are the stars and the black and the white, the blazing, blazing white that is my future. I have the data. I have it right here. There's no protocol for turning back.

And yet. Here is a ladybird.

For You, I Am

Alison Woodhouse, winner, 2019 National Flash Fiction Day Microfiction Competition

For you, I am

afraid
I'll hate your little feet when I fight to put your woollen tights on and you'll grab my hair and pull until I'm sharp and nasty and sound like my mother and I'm
afraid
you'll swallow your new fledged words and learn to hide away from me and I'm
afraid
I'll listen for less than five minutes when you get home from school klaxon-loud and I'm
afraid
you won't get a degree or a job and I'm
afraid
history is circular
but
you've hatched under my skin and there's no way of not loving you now.

Glass

Fiona McKay, winner, Cranked Anvil Flash Competition, Nov 2021

Push it down. All the way down. Everything is fine. I can do this. I can.

It's just a test. Mom always says that a test is just to help the teacher see if the teaching is working, or if there are gaps. The test is more about the teacher, not you. She always says that. When she's talking, and I'm sitting in the car beside her, I believe her, and it's the truth. Then we get to school, and I put on my coat and my smile, wave to her, and she takes the truth away with her in the car. I'm left looking for friends as she indicates and pulls away and disappears into the traffic. And then I must go in.

First class; maths. I breathe all the way down to my ankles and turn the page. Everything makes sense in class, the words and numbers flowing. Then we are cut loose, and left to work through the examples, and it's like swimming too far out to sea: the edges become more distant, more indistinct. A wave of panic breaks over me, leaving my sweating fingertips icy against the table; they are as confused as I am.

Breathe. Push it down. Don't let anyone see. Don't let anyone in. Never ask.

What's the worst thing, mom always asks; what's the very worst thing that could happen if you don't know the answer. I don't know, I always mutter back. The truth is, I do know. I can see exactly what happens. The thing is, I'm invisible. Mom wouldn't understand that. I'm made of glass. Light shines through me, catching on my rough edges and shimmering all the colours of the rainbow. Everyone sees the colours, but not the glass. If I change that, if I put up my hand, then the crystal becomes opaque, the colours vanish, and everyone can see how thick and cloudy my brain is. I wake up at night, picturing their clown-faces looming into mine, fairground-loud and leering. Telling me I'm stupid, stupid, stupid. Telling me I'm nothing. If I let the voices in, I'd have to cut the voices out. Better to keep them out. Better to stay light, and bright, like glass.

Breathe.
Breathe.

Breathe.

Jamie has his hand up. Please miss, please sir, please miss. Jamie always has his hand up. There's a small tide of laughter through the room. The teacher gives the class a dead-eye stare and the laughter drifts into the corner. Yes, Jamie? she says, in a very ordinary voice that is calm, and patient. Jamie asks, and she explains, and the air held tight in my lungs flows out, and warmth and understanding flow back into me.

Mom says we all have the same feelings, but I wonder do the clowns come for Jamie in the night? Is he so much braver? Maybe next time, I'll put up my hand. Maybe. The bell rings.

Push it down. All the way down. Five more classes until home-time.

Good For Her

D. Brody Lipton, winner, Reflex Flash Fiction Competition, Winter 2020

Dad tells Mom to feed the damn cat. She obeys but appears hollow. She pads to the garage, gets in the car, and drives away.

Postcards arrive addressed only to me. Dad never reads them, complaining instead to his buddies that he wishes she'd made dinner before going. On a map at school, I trace her movements.

In Ludlow, she works at a Coke bottling plant, stationed beside a broad-faced woman from Ecuador who hasn't seen her daughter in twelve years. "The *drogas.*"

Mom ices cakes at a Pittsfield bakery until the owner burns it down. She sells the car.

There's a mad painter she lives with in Albany, cleaning his house while he pores over canvases in his barn. He licks his paintbrushes instead of washing them.

Years pass. Dad speaks of Mom like he's spitting on the floor. When I look for my hate, I can't find it.

In a Schenectady hotel, Mom befriends a woman in the room next door. That woman is killed by her boyfriend. Mom stays in town to answer the cops' questions.

She waits tables in a Manchester diner. A grown man orders apple pie "all aboard".

When postcards stop coming, Dad says she's probably dead. I imagine Mom camped in the woods north of Burlington, studying with clear eyes the Canadian border, her hair a crown of greying braids.

I'm eating cereal when Mom comes home.

"Where's the cat?" she asks.

I say she ran away.

Mom says, "Good for her."

Granny Smith, Queene

Elisabeth Ingram Wallace, winner, 2020 QuietManDave Prize

Fluorescent men in high-vis vests hang like fruit in the trees.

I want to pluck one.

Slice him in half, peel off his skin, crunch out his eyes.

This first blue sky day of April, a lorry is reversing, and blue sounds like magpies and a chainsaw cutting down apple trees in the Bluebell woods.

An ancient doodle of wilderness, a dark skinny scrap of me, my parents, grandparents' parents, tangling between the cracks.

Next year the wild-flowers will be gone. No more apples, no more Witches' Thimbles. No more nod and bow, no more great tits fighting worms in the dapples. The breeze will not bruise the fruit sweet. There is talk of an apartment block, with parking for eighty cars.

The newspaper calls it progress.

I call it murder.

I wonder if I can kill a man with a kick to his ladder?

The beach below the orchard is full of pottery shards, white and blue, as if the Victorians came here solely to break things, or clumsily drink tea.
Jagged flowers, a curl, a tendril, a pale wash of willow trees, temples wonky against cream cracked sky.
Once I trod on a shard here. I was five, I sliced a tendon, couldn't walk for a month, run for a year.
But where would I run to? This place throbs in my feet.
Then.
Now.
Now, I hold the day flat on my palms, a mosaic around my life line. I walk back up to the trees.
"Hey," I shout
"Hey!"
When you fat-foot down the ladder, yellow-bellied, I pull it out to show you.
A pilchard, still alive.
I hold it by the tail. It swings like the seconds in my Grandfather clock. Still twitching, skin witching silver in the light, sea water dripping lice down my hands.
You back away, chainsaw in hand.
"Do you know," I say—I stare at your pink skin—

"Do you know, that if I make cuts in the right places, I can lift a fish head off and pull out the spine in one?"
"Can I do that with humans?" I say.
"Do you think?"
You run back up that Queene apple tree like a squirrel in a hard-hat, don't you? Don't you, yellow-belly man?
I cook the fish up for dinner, with magic mushrooms from under the trees. Sip Pippin apple cider till I'm pie eyed.
I take my bike lock and chain myself to a Granny Smith tree, mother the earth in my hands, on my knees.
Now, you're coming, fluorescent.
All of you.
I've scattered temples around me, I've drunk from the pilchard, I have a spine in my hand.
Fight me. I'm sea, I'm mushroom, I'm Queene.

Groceries

Tania Hershman, winner, 2019 Writers' HQ Fight Back LGBTQ+ Flash Contest

I want you to make me pregnant.

But we only have eggs, you say.

I take your hand.

We decide to start with fruit. In the supermarket, we examine melons.

I don't know, you say.

They're the shape of it, I say, holding up one that is oval and oh-so-yellow. We neither of us hide the melon under our shirts, although we know we are both thinking of it and because we know we non-stop-laugh ourselves out of the supermarket, down the street and all the way home. (I never giggled until I met you. I never understood the force of its joy.)

We look to smaller fruit but it doesn't satisfy—although you are taken with a blood orange. (I tell you it's because you have red hair. You nod and say you wish I loved it too but you understand that you can't force me. We get ice cream.)

In bed, when we are skin and skin and sheets and

hair and breasts and fucking, hands stroking and sliding, we decide we will move away from fruit and vegetables, it does not need to be edible.

In fact, you say, maybe it was slightly creepy that we could have eaten it.

You could eat babies, I say, because my head works that way.

True, you say, and I love you more for that one word. I sigh, you sigh, those kinds of sighs that are the two of us, the sigh of skin and skin and sheets and hair and breasts and hands in bed.

In the hardware store, we move from hammers and nails to screws (seems appropriate, you say, and once again we laugh ourselves out of the shop. We find it hard to stay in one place, you and I, for laughing.) In the bathroom store, you are taken with a shower head and I fall in love with a clawfoot tub. But this has nothing to do with procreation, we agree. This is simply fittings.

We find her at last, hidden among the soft furnishings on the fourth floor of a department store. I pass her to you and you hold her and we are not laughing.

Yes, you say.

Yes, I say. I press myself to you with her between us.

We will need to make sure we know how to look after her, you say, solemn as lemons.

It will be a learning process, I say, and take your hand, soft as kiwi fruit. We stand, the three of us, until we hear announcements of closing, of making ways to the exit. We take her, you and I, and pay what's needed, and out in the street and down the street and to our home, our sofa, where all is new because of her, where we choose her name, and where we will teach her how to giggle, how to shop, how to know by sniffing when the melon she's looking for is ready to be opened.

How Much Rain Can a Cloud Hold?

Laurie Bolger, winner, Writers HQ' Flash Fiction Competition, Summer 2019

She wants to be the girl in the passenger seat, feet up on the dashboard, playing with the radio while he drives. Outside, the glass is clinging to a thousand little drops. She tries her best to count them before the windscreen wipers quickly flick them off. She watches him squash his eyes at out- of-date signposts and neither of them can admit that they are lost.

    The place hasn't changed much: heating still on the blink, stale biscuits in a chipped jar from the last time they stayed, but she loves making tea this way, placing the grubby tin kettle on the hob, listening for its hiss. They know each other's movements so well. It's this brilliant dance they do; they've been doing it for years. She loves the way he leans himself against the kitchen door; thinks of him reliving his childhood from the back porch. They've come here to remember, in all that November mud.

    Tonight, she'll build the fireplace and won't let him help. They'll play board games with the bits missing, no one will win. She'll sit holding him to her chest like glass, holding grief like the whole house, imagining being able to send grief in an envelope, the weight of it in her hand.

She knows in the morning the clouds will sap the sun and the windows in the house will be wet. She knows they will walk their grief in other people's wellies. Him, taking in the silver lichen trees; her, running and being angry at him for standing still.

When the fire burns out. They go upstairs. Flop into a bed that's damp with cold. Him worrying about grey hairs, her worrying about ghosts. She decides it doesn't matter where they go. Grief will follow. Even in the sunniest places it won't dry itself out of them.

They are piles of wet washing with nowhere to hang themselves out.

He buys fat mushrooms from the supermarket, rich in vitamin D. After the mushrooms, they walk in silence, this time by the drip of a stream. She tells him that swans mate for life and he gives her a look as lonely as the sky.

She moves her hand across the bed sheets. They're like the ones she had as a kid. She remembers the clean smell when her Mum tucked the corners in, her pretending the bed was an island, the carpet the sea.

She pushes her face to his shoulder and hears him breathe. She wipes her nose on his sleeve. She wants to wake him up.

There's this painting on the wall of two parrots with pastel-coloured wings. She imagines them flying, but they are leaning on each other like two worn out trees, knowing that if one of them gets up to leave, well, that'll be it.

I Found Myself Lost

Pauline Masurel, winner, 2021 Gloucestershire Writers' Network Prose Prize

The year it happened was the year that I moved into my own head.

The relocation was only intended to be temporary, a matter of lugging in a small daybed with a mountain of cushions and an old quilt. I took my knitting, some books and a few embroidered homilies to install on the uneven walls. It was cramped but cosy. Until I discovered that I could roll back the ceilings to create rooms of infinite height.

I painted my cerebrum in Dulux Elise silk emulsion. I chose flock wallpaper and wood panelling for the hippocampus, giving it the atmosphere of a country inn snug (pre smoking ban). I added an enormous glitterball of sunshine in the cerebellum and obtained free-range skylarks as house pets. These took off vertically from the crop-stubble carpet and flew so high that I could no longer see the trembling specks of their bodies.

Once I had realised my mind was so deceptively spacious there was no going back. I engaged a house clearance company to dispose of my other belongings and put my house on the market. I kept little from my old life and furnished this new intracranial sanctuary from my own imagination, with a few frivolous accessories from IKEA.

I went through a phase of staging stadium concerts: Springsteen, U2, Pink Floyd and others performed. I had the advantage that I could book them at the peak of their careers. You can debate amongst yourself which years I had in mind. I wasn't pedantic about this, allowing myself the luxury of up to three anachronistic numbers in their encores and a support band from any era or genre; the more incongruous the billing the better. This was fun but after a couple of weeks I realised it wasn't conducive to getting anything else done. So I developed a penchant for religious vocal music instead, spanning the gamut of Gregorian chants, Sufi singing and gospel choirs.

I probably should have realised that it wouldn't last forever. Perhaps if I had seen the change coming I would have invited others to share the comfort and spectacle of a life lived inside my own brain. Hindsight is both a wonderful and dispiriting thing.

I felt safe and secure. The only indication that things were not as they should be was a slight ground tremor which woke me one morning. I lay in the dark uncertainty. I raised the lighting to observe what might have altered. There were fresh flowers in the vases and some intriguing items of post had appeared. Everything was clean and there was the faintest hint of lemon and vanilla. It was warm but not stuffy. There was a breeze, yet no chill. If my mind had been a potting compost then it would have been "free-draining and moisture-retentive." So far, so very usual.

But things were not normal, not even "normal for now." My den had acquired a new doorway in the night, one which opened straight onto a terrace that had not been there before, from which a series of steps led to a broad lawn and a gravel driveway that passed between an avenue of trees to an enormous wrought iron gate. My first thought was "who put those there?" which was foolish, since nothing ever happened thereabouts which wasn't entirely of my own making. For a few weeks I ignored the changes. By day I concentrated on baking scones, practising the flute and learning Italian. At dusk I lit the firepit barbecue and watched the glow-worms.

Every morning, the route out of my mind persisted, still leading to who knew where.

I don't know what eventually prompted me. There was nothing in particular to distinguish the day on which I finally left from any of the other days on which I lived there. One morning I rose, showered and dressed. Without packing, I left the key on the hall table, walked out of the door, across the terrace and down the steps. I crunched along the gravel drive to reach the gate. At the end of the driveway there stood a wooden fingerpost, pointing the way out. At that moment I felt as though it was the sign I had been waiting for all my life.

Only when the gate was firmly shut behind me could I read the lettering. Carved into the weathered wooden surface was the simple legend, "All Routes."

If a Tree Falls

Rachel O'Cleary, winner, Strands International Flash Fiction Competition, Sept 2020

Her
She grips the rough bark between her knees, grunting as she reaches higher, hands already pink and stinging. Splinters pierce her palms and thighs, but she continues, eyes reaching up, only up.

She stops. This is it. This is the one. She hoists one leg over the branch and stretches—head out, toes curled against the trunk.

The branch wobbles, but she hugs it tightly, inhaling earthy bark and tangy orange leaf. Her heart stops walloping and settles instead into a smooth roll. She rests, eyes half-open, and breathes with the tree. In. Out. In.

Them
Mum is nowhere to be seen. Her car is in the driveway, but no healthy snack awaits them on the table, no strident voice orders them out of their uniforms.

Their calls race round corners and up stairs.

It is the boy who finds her, being just young enough to think of looking for his mother in a tree. His sister doesn't believe him, but not knowing what else to do, she finally comes. Her eyes, round and clear as bubbles, rise to meet her mother's.

The boy giggles and shrieks at Mummy's game, but the girl only tilts her head. Her body stills, as if she is approaching a stray cat.

"It's OK, Mum," she coos. "You can come down now."

Mum grips the tree tighter and twitches her head slightly. Her eyes rest on the children for a moment, then close.

Him

He finds them sitting beneath the tree, chins tilted up. The boy is no longer having fun. He wipes the tears from his pink cheeks with his sleeve, so Dad won't see.

They tell him they have begged, promised good behaviour, even tried to tempt her down with chocolate.

He cranes his neck.

"Come on now," he calls. "What are you playing at? Look at the children—who will take care of them?"

She meets his stare, but says nothing, moves not a millimetre.

"Shit," he says. Goes to the shed.

When he returns, saw in hand, the girl jumps up, pushes against him frantically.

"No!" she shouts. "No, leave her! I'll make dinner. I'll put him to bed. Just leave her!"

He brushes past.

The chainsaw roars to life, and he stands holding it, watching his wife in the tree. Waiting. She doesn't blink.

He finds the crotch in the tree that holds up her branch and presses the blade in. The whine of the saw becomes a deep growl. A puff of pale sawdust leaps from the tree and softly floats down to earth. He withdraws, pauses again. The children wail, mouths open, but he cannot hear them. His eyes lock on hers.

Blade returns to branch, woodchips flying in all directions. The roaring and swirling mounts as the blade pushes further. A pale dust sticks to their skin, their sweat, their tears. And then, a sharp crack.

Her eyes cool and placid, even as she falls.

In the Car

Bernadette M. Smyth, winner, 2009 Fish One-Page Story Prize

I steered through fantastic streets of boisterous traffic, past glittering buildings, and footpaths that moved with shoppers. I beeped the horn when I saw Mrs Sweeney.

"Hop in!" I shouted.

"The town's mad," she said, getting into the car.

"Packed! There's hundreds in town."

"*Thousands* more like."

"*Millions* even—I'd say there's easily a million people doing their shopping today."

Mrs Sweeney tightened her headscarf.

"Plenty of groceries there," I said.

"Sure haven't I ten mouths to feed, Petulia?"

"Ten kids? That's nothing—I've fifteen."

"Humph! If I only had fifteen children I'd be laughing—I've *twenty* you know."

"You said ten!"

"No, no, Petulia, ten *at the moment*: John-Joe, Jimmy, Jamesy, Jemmy, Mary-Concepta, Concepta-Mary, Penelope, Agnes, Ignatius, and Alphonsus, are away on their holidays."

I went back to the steering.

"How's Paddy's leg?" I enquired.

"Gone."

"Gone?"

"Chopped off!"

"And how does he manage?"

"Sure he has to hop!"

"God, that's desperate!"

"It is, Petulia, especially with twenty children knocking him over."

"Still," I said, "isn't it better to be missing a leg than have an extra one. There's my Johnny and he's awful bother with the three legs."

"Three? That's nothing—I've a brother with four."

"Four legs, Mrs Sweeney?"

"Four—he has to crawl so he does."

"And has he a tail?"

"No…"

Mrs Sweeney's voice collapsed as she looked towards the house. Mammy was standing at the kitchen window. "I've told you two already!" she shouted, "No playing in the car! GET INSIDE NOW!"

Michelle scrambled out of the car, leaving behind

Mrs Sweeney and her phantom groceries, Paddy and Johnny, and the village of characters who lived somewhere between the car's upholstery and our imaginations.

    I ran after her, over the path, and into the house where our tea was waiting.

La Loba

Vicki Jarrett, winner, 2018 Shoreline of Infinity Magazine Flash Competition

We thought we'd be safer away from the city. And, for the most part, we were right. Staying there would've been madness, but survival out here does involve sacrifice.

High up in one of the taller trees at the edge of a clearing, we get as comfortable as we can in its wide, spreading branches. The moon is rising round and full into the night sky, claiming its place among the stars. It'll be a long night. Hank stretches out with exaggerated weariness, his back the same width as the branch he's lying on. One false move is all it'd take. When I suggest he move to a safer position he sighs, shifts his shoulders a fraction and closes his eyes. Shadows gather in the lines and hollows of his face while moonlight silvers the surface, giving him the look of a tarnished icon.

It's been four weeks since Nina's last episode. We had hoped, once we were free of the hysteria gripping the city, that maybe she'd somehow be cured. Naive perhaps, but it was better than letting them take her and put her in one of those treatment facilities along with all the other girls. The ones they could catch. They say they're working on a cure. But how can that be, when they don't even know what caused the disease in the first place, or why it spread exclusively among the adolescent female population?

We never thought it would happen to our Nina. She was such a sweet child. At first it was the moods, the slammed doors, the way she'd snarl at us if we asked a simple question about schoolwork or friends. We learned to recognise the signs and back off. Well, I did. Hank never did know when to leave well alone. It was a language he couldn't, or wouldn't, begin to understand.

She started staying out late. We'd wait up, worried sick. When she came back she refused to explain herself, would fly into a rage and shut herself in her room, leaving a trail of muddy footprints through the house. The next day she'd be pale and withdrawn. She never made any effort to hide her torn and bloody clothes, simply cramming them into the laundry basket for me to wash. Hank thought this was just typical selfish behaviour but I believed it was her way of telling me what was happening to her, of asking for my help.

I stare out across the clearing, my attention snagged by movement at the edge of the wood, where the trees thicken. It could be Nina, or it could be one of the others. A substantial number of girls must have made it out of the cities as well as us. In the weeks we've been surviving out here, we've seen the signs. The blackened smudges of camp fires, shelters made from fallen branches, scattered bones.

It took me months to convince Hank we needed to leave or risk losing her altogether. He talked about his job at the council, about the mortgage on the house. Since we left, his grumbling about the day to day hardships we face has made me wonder whether he wouldn't rather have handed Nina over to the authorities and carried on with his life as though she'd never happened. I don't want to believe that, but his recent speculation that they might have cracked the science and developed a safe, viable cure by now, that it could be safe to go back, has done nothing to quieten my doubts about his priorities.

The movement in the trees comes again, from what seems to be several different places at once. There's definitely more than one of them in there. Sounds like a fight. My heart races and I have to push down the instinct to run to my daughter's defence. That wouldn't help anyone. And anyway, I can't really know whether those growling sounds are aggressive or friendly. Perhaps they're finding each other, all these lost girls, seeking strength in numbers.

The hours pass and I watch the moon cross the sky. In her light, the silver edges of the world are rivers that swell and contract, joining and separating again, always in motion. Hank murmurs in his sleep and goes to roll over. Before he manages to tip out of the tree, he is saved by some unconscious sense of balance and rights himself again. All without opening his eyes.

The moon is sinking now, the night nearly over. A pale shape is weaving through the trees, coming in our direction. Never before has she shown herself before dawn, when she usually reappears, in one piece if slightly dazed. But I've never seen her like this. I hold my breath, stay very still, and watch my daughter emerge from the shadows.

The powerful, fluid way she moves, the way her body seems to shine, not only with unmistakable health but with the same unflinching clarity as the moon. My breath escapes in a gasp. My god. She's magnificent.

How can this be a disease? Who gets to decide? Those sick old men in lab coats, injecting healthy girls with their so-called cure in their treatment centres?

She draws close and circles our tree, looking up through the branches with gleaming eyes. Even without Hank's snoring and twitching, she'd have found us. We're connected. She makes a low anxious whining noise from the back of her throat and somehow I know she hasn't fed tonight. And she must. Evolution is hungry work.

Perhaps it was always going to come to this. For every step forward there must be a shedding of what came before. I flex my feet, easing the stiffness out of my ankles, stretch out my legs and press them close to Hank's, feeling his familiar warmth. One false move is all it'd take.

Last, Best Hope in a Shade of Orange
Taria Karillion, winner, Flash500 competition, Feb 2021

To: Audit Officer 5688A
You are assigned to audit the randomly selected subjects detailed in previous memos. Preliminary reports suggest termination of subjects failing to meet quality standards.

From: GN [Accounts]
Have either of you met this Auditor? Rumour is he's a bit 'eccentric'.
Management are as nervous as turkeys at Christmas.
PS: New drinks machine on 4th floor—ABOUT TIME!

From: SC [Tech Support]
He's been here all day, breathing down our necks and mumbling into a dictaphone without a word to us—rude! Reckon evil overlords at HQ planning to give some of us the chop? Grr! :-(

From: GN [Accounts]
I've only heard him muttering at the drinks machine in

some foreign language. I tell you he is *weird*—I don't like his shifty eyes (The Eighties called—they want their coloured contacts back! And talk about false tan o*range*—it's like being in an old Tango advert! #POSER!)

From: YF [Mailroom]
Don't be so catty u guys—he's probably harmless. Ok, fake tan & funky contacts not so GR8, but maybe he's a shortsighted ace ballroom dancer? U never know if u don't make an effort 2 B friendly! He might B interesting 2 talk 2 if he's from Ukraine or Iceland or wherever. Let's ask him 2 join us 4 coffee break?

From: GN [Accounts]
I prefer my Cappuccino *without* a garnish of eavesdropping weirdo, thanks.
Speaking of coffee—that damn machine is *still* out of order—hasn't worked since it arrived!!

From: SC [IT]
Sounds like *you*, G! LOL. Know what you mean, though—I think he's been listening in to my calls—creepy! >:-(

From: YF [Mailroom]

U R *mean* girlies! He was here earlier 2day and I saw him pick up all the courier's dropped parcels, listen 2 the cleaner's ramblings, fix the hand drier in the gents & even water the dying plants...bless! I gave him a cuppa and showed him how 2 high 5, and he actually smiled back! B *nice* 2 the poor guy—maybe he's just shy and doesn't get out much?

Now I'm off 2 THUMP the drinks machine until it gives me hot chocolate :-)

From: HR, Head Office

Please accept our apologies for the delay in sending our Auditor—her visit has had to be rescheduled for next week.

From: Audit Officer 56887A
To: Monitoring Post 349

Final audit of randomly selected subjects complete.

Contrary to all initial reports, evidence of sustained benevolence has been found.

Recommend suspension of Malevolent Species Termination Order.

Urgent request: Inter-dimensional transport pod is in need of immediate repair—critical damage sustained to outer hull by indigenous life-forms believing it to be a beverage dispenser.

--- *END* ---

Lessons in Attachment Parenting
Sara Hills, winner, Flash Fiction Festival Showstopper Challenge, June 2021

I cull through your belongings for a recent photo and find everything but. You at thirty, dark hair in pin curls, cigarette jabbed between pale lips, your hands blocking half your face from the camera. You at twenty, facing the gray-green sea. You at twelve, in faded dungarees with your tongue out.

You never liked having your picture taken. You joked you'd lose your soul.

Now, the mortician teases your limp hair, lipsticks your mouth so you become even more of a stranger. Black dress against white satin. Dark hair against waxen skin.

Does your mother look okay? he asks, as if I'm attached.

I shrug.

When it's my turn to say goodbye, your name hangs sharp on my tongue.

*

You don't want the children calling you Grandma. *Why can't they call me by my actual name?* you ask.

Mark's mother is a real Granny. When she monologues about the benefits of baby-wearing and breastfeeding, you roll your eyes. She rocks the babies in the green glider chair, reads fairy books and sings hushing lullabies while you hold back.

The best decision you ever made, you say, was teaching me to self-soothe.

*

At sixteen, I'm the same age as you were when you had me. The same pouting bottom lip, the same slender hips. If I knew what was good for me, you say, I'd focus on school. Become somebody.

Your teeth snap around the words. But what do you know?

The warmth from being wanted consumes me, completes me, then overtakes me.

You drive me to the clinic, saying, *It's just a mass of cells. Better to take care of it before you become attached.*

You sign the papers but won't wait for me inside. I tell myself I don't want you to.

*

On my first day of kindergarten, you hold my hand. You point out the primary-colored posters on the walls—the alphabeted animals (A is for Alligator) and the days of the week (Today is Monday). I cling to your legs, my tiny fists grasping at the slick knit fabric of your slacks, and one-by-one the teacher pries my fingers away.

It's for the best, the teacher tells you. *You don't want her getting too attached.*

When you slip away from me, latching the heavy door between us, I come undone—hands thrashing, breath hitching—the name "Mama" catching in the snot of my throat.

Lost Appetite

Bean Sawyer, winner, Globe Soup Microfiction Challenge, Sept 2021

She watched as he tucked into the grub.

She'd spent hours preparing the meal down to every meticulous detail: the honey glaze on the carrots, the crisp of the roast potatoes, the soft rise of the Yorkshire pudding—the tender cut of the beef. Hours spent in the kitchen that she'll never get back.

Seven wasted years. And there he was, diving in like William the Conqueror—stuffing his face, talking while chewing, licking his knife, slurping gravy from his plate.

"You not eating, love?"

She poured herself a large glass of Bordeaux.

"I'm not hungry," she said.

Morning Routine

Kim Catanzarite, winner, 2020 Fish Flash Fiction Prize

I opened a can of cat food and grabbed a saucer and one of the forks nobody likes and scooped out the food and gave the fat one the fork to lick and gave the kitten the full saucer and lifted their water dishes from the floor and filled them up and then turned the lights on in the living room and raised the blinds in the eating area and made my way to the fridge and put the bread in the toaster and grabbed the butter before tapping out the allergy medicine and her ADHD medicine and her other allergy medicine and pouring her glass of water. Then I put the kettle on and grabbed the brush and dustpan and picked up some mud that tracked in on her shoes the night before, and then the toast popped and I buttered it and she came in and said "good morning" and asked me if her socks matched her outfit and I said yes and she told me it was cold outside and that she was going to freeze her ass off at the bus stop if I didn't drive her there, and I told her that she would live, and she breathed out a cloud of disgust and said that if the puddle down the road was enormous like it was the other day I would have to drive her because she couldn't get around it, it was so big, and I stared at her and said nothing because that's often the best response, and then she looked out the window and also said nothing, so I knew the puddle was gone.

Mouse

Gillian O'Shaughnessy, winner, Reflex Flash Fiction Competition, Autumn 2020

Grandma ate poison five times before it killed her. It was hard to keep it down, but she persisted. She went mad, they said, because of the isolation, she couldn't hack it, she was a city girl after all, an intellectual, she came to life at parties, she smoked and wore high-neck lace dresses and polished button boots, she danced with slick suit boys, not third sons out riding the boundaries checking the fences for months and months.

She ate the shouting in her head; she ate her shrieking heart. She ate the crashing silence of the endless outside, with only the grizzle of grey-backed sheep and the whine of flies for relief. On bad days she'd walk miles to the top of the long dirt driveway and back again, to the hot dust that turned her sheets and dresses brown and the ochre-coloured everything that stretched for days and days.

She ate the loneliness she wasn't meant to notice. She ate boredom straight from the packet and stopped remembering why she really should get a plate. No-one to care if she did or she didn't. No-one to drink gin with on the veranda. No-one to discuss the newspapers that came months too late, just a mirror of women with blank faces she saw once a year at shearing time when they came to help with the cooking for hours and hours.

Grandma ate poison five times before it killed her. Some women would do that before they'd leave their husbands and their children because if there is too much of you, if you can't swallow your panic that this is everything there'll ever be, all you can do, all there is to do, is become smaller and smaller.

Mum Died

Rowena Warwick, winner, 2020 Bridport Flash Fiction Prize

Mum died reaching for a packet on the top shelf of a kitchen cupboard. She died cleaning out the rabbit hutch, and again after a dog ate Hazel. I was sitting on the back-doorstep shelling peas when it happened. Somehow, I wasn't surprised. She died again when her car ran into a stationary vehicle, you remember? We were on the way home from ballet in Harlow, that man shouted but it didn't matter because mum was dead. She died in the pub while we were sitting outside with our crisps and once more singing at church, where there was a pillar and we couldn't see her. Before all this she had died several times in Dad's Ford Anglia when he was teaching her to drive, luckily it was only her. Later she died when I got my A level results, a grand death with histrionics and proper flowers. She died in those shoes which were the wrong colour on my wedding day and frequently since in the photos. She died with the arrival of each grandchild, there have been six, or perhaps she was already dead having suffered through each delivery. She died magnificently when she retired and again at the bungalow, such a lovely garden, the pond, the tree heavy with plums. But more recently she has used it all up, her skill in dying. Thin as a wisp she lies, grasping the covers as if she might fall, as if death might not be able to catch her.

Mum's the Word
Valerie O'Riordan, winner, 2010 Bristol Short Story Prize

Three times with his grunting and the calloused hand over my mouth: first, the kitchen wall rough at my back; second, hands and knees against the splintered attic floor; third, pushing me into the thin mattress, while my mother slept in the next room, her belly swollen and taut. Then a sticky wrap of silver paper, chocolate to slip into my pocket on the way to school. Hands and legs all sticky, and neither of us speaking.

When the time came, they rammed a tongs between my mother's legs, but all they got out was a tangled grey-face thing that took a single half-hearted breath. My mother was split open. I heard her screaming. Later I helped my aunts boil the bedsheets: we scoured and bleached them, but finally they sent me out to dump them in the skip in the back alley. I bundled the rest up too, the stained knickers and the ripped tights, wrapped them up in the pillowcase where nobody would see. I crouched in the dark beside the metal bin and vomited, a watery spew all over my good shoes. He was watching me from the kitchen window when I came back up the path, my hand on my stomach. He said, it's the two of us now, girl, and held me by the shoulder. His face was red and wet.

When I couldn't go to school any more, the clothes straining to cover me, my armpits stained with the sweat of my bulk, he left me alone. My shadow on the bedroom wall in the moonlight was like the moon itself, round and still. I heard him coming in when the light was trickling over the treetops, his steps back and forth in the corridor, his sobbing through the wall. My aunts had stopped visiting when he stopped letting them inside; I sweated and pushed on my own, and the baby screamed. He had it brought away; the social worker shook her head as she swaddled it and said love, a big girl like you, didn't you take precautions? His arm around my shoulder, fingers kneading, as he said, I'll keep a better eye on her, Miss, don't you worry.

Never Let Me Go

Cathy Lennon, winner, 2014 National Flash Fiction Day Microfiction Contest

First it was cartons and tins on the worktops, then newspapers on the stairs. Each window-sill sparkled with tin foil. He made me a necklace of ring-pulls and bottle tops. Like swans we perched on our bundles of rags and flattened boxes, smoothing the creases from wrappers. The hallway was Manhattan, a canyon of towering piles. Across the no man's land in our bedroom our fingertips would touch, until one day they couldn't anymore. From the other side, perplexed, he watched the tears slide down my face. He threw me two empty film canisters to catch them in.

One of the Girls

Monica Dickson, winner, 2019 Northern Short Story Festival Flash Slam

The boys call her Wardy, like she's one of the lads, a bit of a laugh. Maybe she's leading a double life; they all fancy her anyway. They just ignore me, most of the time. Same goes for the teachers. Jane Ward's intelligent and independent. I'm invisible.

I do everything with my best mate, Carmen. We walk to school and tennis club and Guides and that keeps us on the right side of the good girls, even if we do smoke on the way. So I should have known better than to go round Harriet's without Car. Jane Ward is already there, lying on the bed in Harriet's room, reading. Wordy Wardy. She sends a half-arsed nod in my direction; her bob sways back and forth either side of her jaw, like abandoned swings. I collapse onto a beanbag in a fake swoon; Harriet laughs. I think she likes me—why else would she invite me? Not sure about her dad though. When I arrive he doesn't speak, just holds the door open so I have to duck under his arm to get past. He smells of Imperial Leather and last night's booze. I keep my head down and stomp up the stairs. At the top I look back and he's still standing there, giving me a funny look. I say *tiny cock* under my breath, which is something I've worked out you can do without moving your lips. And filthy ventriloquism is a talent of sorts.

The afternoon gapes, like Saturdays do, and we loll about listening to records. Harriet and Jane talk to each other and I talk to Harriet and try to make her laugh again. Harriet's got a new album and the two of us sing along and act sad and sexy, like we're in a video. Jane drifts about, not joining in. A hard ball of empty forward rolls in my belly, like I'm hungry or homesick, even though I'd rather be anywhere but. It's the same with people; I hate Jane Ward but I still want her to like me. Then I remember how she likes the sound of her own voice and I have this idea that we should make a tape of the three of us messing about. Jane gets all enthusiastic then and we spend ages recording what we're going to do that day; go Asda, go swimming, go round the ring road on the number 9, even though none of us have got any money or swimming costumes and it's already four o'clock and starting to get dark.

It's quiet for a bit and I'm trying not to think about having to go back and I'm staring at the red light on the stereo, listening to the far away squeak of the tape as it strains on pause. Then I just start talking gibberish about being a Victorian maid. I don't know why, it just comes out of my mouth and I jump up and start pretending to dust the room and asking, "Ew are you two?" and "What's this new-fangled machine what yer playing with?" I keep it up for ages and my voice gets higher and sillier and I start chucking stuff round the room.

It's supposed to be funny and Harriet's wetting herself but Jane Ward starts getting radged, she goes to me, "Stop it Nicole, you're freaking me out" and even though her face is still as smug as the Mona Lisa's I know she actually is bricking herself. Harriet's still cackling away though and her braces are catching on what's left of the light so her teeth look like that James Bond villain. I say, "You should be freaked out, look at Harriet's face" and Harriet laughs even more in this sort of screechy, Halloween-y way and then Wardy starts proper blubbing and I say, in my best witchy voice, "Why are you crying little girl?" and loom right up in her face and she shouts, really loud, "Get off me you nutter!"

That's when Harriet's dad walks in. He doesn't knock; he just puts the light on and says in a really calm, smooth voice like he's a presenter off the telly, "What are you young ladies up to in here?" Harriet goes red and says, "Nothing, Dad" which is technically true. He looks at Jane Ward's white, teary face, then at me, all out of breath, hair stuck to my forehead. He says, "Time to go home now, don't you think" and I know he means me and it's not a question.

    I try to get my tongue round *fuck off*, silently, without moving my lips. It's impossible.

Plum Jam

Frances Gapper, Winner, 2018 Flashback Fiction Microfiction Contest

From our ladders we can see the plum-blue Malverns. The army's bought up this harvest, still on the trees. We pickers are a crew: boy scouts, gypsies, PoWs, refugees, us girls in our mackintosh skirts and hurden aprons. Blue for canning and bottling, yellow to Ticklers jam factory in Grimsby. Tommies eat plum, our Joe says. "What d'you want with eggs and ham when you've got plum and apple jam?" Sergeants get the raspberry, higher up the strawberry and blackcurrant. We're feeding our boys, helping the war effort. Lots goes to waste, though —fallen, smashed, rotting where it lies.

Polio

Nicholas Ruddock, winner, 2013 Bridport Flash Fiction Prize

In 1953 the polio virus hovered over the summertime streets of Toronto, it multiplied in the warmth of slow-moving creeks and in the shallow sands of Ward's Island, in rainfall it slipped down from the canopy of maple, elm, heat and cicadas, vaporizing into random bedrooms thought secure, tasteless on the tongues of those who lay commingled there. Over breakfast we heard radio accounts of children slumped like rags, breathless, cyanotic, living out their lives within relentless metal carapaces, "iron lungs" pushing, pulling at the paralyzed chest itself incapable of moving air, and those children who had been rendered voiceless by tracheotomy used their teeth to go *click-click-click* drawing the attention of nurses to their plight (real or imagined) and the *click-click-clicking* ratcheted up as the sky darkened with ozone and thunder and the threat of power failure which would bring parents, neighbours and passers-by unimpeded to the open wards in a rush of fear-of-smothering, the starch white dresses of the nurses "like moths" amidst the to-and-fro swishing of tubes, the children lying as though beheaded, the sick quarantined, the healthy (you and I) taken to the cedar-filled air of Inverhuron where the second of the Great Lakes beat against a series of reefs straight out from shore, where in the last shelf of rock (before the lake dropped off to what seemed to us to be fathoms of darkness) we could see the petrified coral bodies of tiny crustaceans, locked into their airless world centuries before polio.

Press 3 for Random Track
Dri Chiu Tattersfield, winner, 2022 Blue Frog Flash Fiction Contest

It is 3:00AM and 告白氣球 by Jay Chou comes on the karaoke machine.

 I am not at the 24-hr Holiday KTV in Zhonghe on Jingxin Street, with its dim yellow lighting and glorious two-tiered soda machine. I am not leaning against Liu-ayi as she belts the lyrics with three times the intensity of the original, pretending to sleep so Mom won't say it's too late for a ten-year-old to be up and make me go home. My other aunties are not on their phones, rolling their eyes but smiling at Liu-ayi's high notes.

 Instead, I am on the floor of my apartment in LA, staring at the karaoke jukebox I bought off Craigslist five hours ago. Photos on Google Maps open beside me show that the Holiday KTV has been thoroughly renovated with purple neon lights and a full bar. My chest is a pit. I am an outline of myself. And Liu-ayi has been missing for three days.

 爸我回來了 comes on next. The other aunties would pause during the rap parts but Liu-ayi always took them on, bars committed to memory. Something feels different about the sound from the jukebox, like it's coming from inside my head, but I'm distracted. I mouth the words as the family LINE group chat I've had muted for years buzzes with messages:

Liu-meimei has been going to strange bars lately.
No, she's always done that.
She came home on the back of a suspicious tall woman's motorcycle last Tuesday, very late!
Has she been taking drugs?
She should have a boyfriend to protect her. Look what's happened now! Where is she??

I frown. I cannot imagine her doing any of these things.

Liu-ayi always sang romantic songs the loudest, even though, as the other aunties pointed out, she had never had a boyfriend. She wasn't technically the youngest, but everyone called her mei-mei. At her younger sister's wedding Liu-ayi cried onstage and promised, "I'll be next!" After we got home I kneeled behind the dehumidifier, the holiest place in the house, and prayed she wouldn't so she could keep taking me to karaoke forever.

In the dark, I crouch in front of the jukebox and press VIDEO as the guzheng notes of 雨下一整晚 twang in my ear. The whole jukebox flickers for a moment, and my hand passes through as if it were a projection. I pull back, then shake my head—my dissociation acting up. A grainy Jay Chou blinks onto the screen, crooning in a cream-colored satin suit.

As I got older, I started staring at the lyrics during weekly karaoke, willing them to move faster. I sensed a distance separating me from my family, so I widened and solidified it; better a chasm I could see clearly than a small gap I could trip over. Soon, Liu-ayi's earnestness curdled in my mouth like over-sweetened soymilk. I came to karaoke less and less.

The music crackles to a stop. My thighs prickle with numbness. The screen flashes:

ALBUM END

PRESS 1 FOR MAIN MENU

PRESS 2 TO PLAY AGAIN

PRESS 3 FOR RANDOM TRACK

I have work in four hours. I press 3.

雨下一整晚 begins to play again, and the camera zooms in on a white-suited figure. I am about to shuffle again when I pause. The figure in the music video is shorter than before, with hair dyed a reddish brown instead of Jay Chou's black and centimeters away from a pixie cut. I press my laptop to my face until I can inhale the pixels, but I am already sure:

Liu-ayi is on the screen.

She rocks against the microphone stand, closes her eyes. My stomach crumples. Then unfolds: *She is. Here?* A tall woman in a black leather jacket walks into frame. The camera pans out and they slow-dance, Liu-ayi caressing the woman's long hair, and Liu-ayi is also still in the corner with the microphone stand, and also behind everyone, older, greying, strumming a blue guitar. *A-yi.* There are seven of her, eight, overlapping, fading in and out of each other: a teenager shaving her head, an elderly couple making egg pancakes. *Here.* In grainy color the jukebox displays an entire life all at once.

After years without song my mouth begins to move.

The screen's edges slip open and so do mine. The room tilts and I fall forward, somehow calm—nothing has felt real since her disappearance, but this does. Weightless, I pass through the screen like a ray of light. Liu-ayi's face flickers between hers and my own. I once would have been revulsed at our merging but now I reach forward, trying to grasp her face, mine. My body resonates with music, a medium for the soundwaves. Faint outlines of my apartment float around us, my life layered beneath this joint space. Fingers blink. Turn translucent. I always knew we shared something, but was horrified by the way Liu-ayi threw herself into our family over and over; I wanted to come into myself on my own. I put on the white suit jacket, grab the microphone and sing. In my body and outside of it, I watch myself with love. Sound and color flood me. I am fuller than I have ever been.

    My throat strains as I sing louder, sliding out of key. In the jukebox I watch us sway, wheel, laugh. My apartment's outlines begin to solidify but the jukebox-world only brightens, all of my worlds real at once. Pixels glitter and we move with the freedom I always sought by detaching. Pale purple light begins to filter into the window and I scream, I scream-

***

In a private karaoke room in Kaohsiung, two women duet 告白氣球 by Jay Chou. The TV screen switches to a figure kneeling by a window at sunrise, belting 雨下一整晚.

    "There you are, little Wen." The shorter one smiles.

Recesses

Brenden Layte, winner, 2021 The Forge Literary Magazine Flash Competition

You're eight or nine and you can barely fit in the pantry because it's mostly taken up by a broken washer and dryer that have been broken since they've been here. The kind of detritus that people pick up thinking they'll fix it one day but things never really ever get fixed, and so you're climbing on them to grab a can of Beefaroni and maybe a Devil Dog for after, and this seems good even though your mom is mad that you drink too much soda and eat too much "crap" when you're here, but your father wasn't allowed to have treats when he was a kid, even when he wasn't being beaten, and so he has snacks everywhere, and you have asthma and you're breathing in cigarette smoke and the sliding wooden doors to the front room are shut and sealed because heat is too expensive in the winter, but there's something comforting here for moments at a time.

Years later you might realize that there's something about eating trash, or something that somebody might consider trash, or something somebody might consider the kind of thing that somebody who is trash would eat, and there's especially something about it if you're doing it under threat of ridicule ("Aren't you going to fucking eat?") or self-recrimination (*You piece of shit. This is disgusting.*), but some people grow up eating a lot of food out of cans and maybe some were picky eaters, but also maybe it was just how it was and there was a warmth to the simplicity and it doesn't really mean you're bad and shouldn't be here even if right now you're in a house with a carved wooden bannister and a fainting couch that you would've called a mansion when you were a kid and these people around you now somehow consider something like a middle class home even though the poorest of them makes six figures and you used to think middle class was like 30k a year because at least you weren't on welfare.

    You only should have had the two drinks you said you'd have before eating, but you knew you wouldn't, so you wonder why you even say things like that so you can be disappointed in yourself later. And now everybody knows that you apparently missed the *Boeuf en Croûte* step from trash to respectable enough to be here, and since you're the type of person to have a master's degree in linguistics but never not laugh at the French word for *beef*, now they also all know that you didn't know you could even put steak in a pastry, and they all know that you don't know French (and aren't even the type of person who can put on a French accent to say food the right way), and also you tried to be funny and make a Beefaroni joke that turned into an anecdote when nobody laughed, and so they all know that you lived on a steady diet of canned pasta when you were a kid, and also "Oh my god, how could they smoke with you inside?"

So, you slip away and stop and look at the stairs because you don't know what else to do and you wonder why the recesses on old wood bannisters are always the darkest part. Does it dry that way or do people go through the trouble of using different types of stain on different parts of the railing, or is it just a trick of light? Maybe the darkest coating just flows into the deepest recesses and then if people's fingers can't reach in there, or just don't, it settles that way like silt, but you'd think that people like this would really try to get in there and keep things nice even if only for appearance's sake in that appearance is still a consideration and not something just drawn on and then drawn from so that everybody knows who you should be really nice to and who you can be just a little rude to and who you're allowed to forget the second you turn away from them.

      You're at the part of the night where somebody will notice your arm when you reach for something or adjust your shirt for at least the tenth time too many and they'll want to talk about their tattoos and ask about yours and you'll demur or find an excuse to leave the room because you've established that this isn't a place for even joking earnestness and we're not doing this, but if you can't get away, you can drink faster and maybe by the time they finish the story about their family crest or the flower they used to pick with their grandmother or whatever, you'll be drunk enough to say that your mother cried when you came home with your first tattoo and it's covered up now because sometimes 17-year-olds do things they don't agree with later, and there's a joke in there about making your mother cry for no reason and it's not funny, but you can't mention most of what you were up to from the ages of like 16 to 28 in your current company anyways, and we're not doing this, but now the thing that made your mother cry is covered by what the person you're talking to caught a glimpse of, which is the head of a Laotian demon that you saw a monument of when you were on day whatever of an opium binge in Vientiane, and entered the demon's mouth into the darkness of hell and climbed and climbed up these pitch-black stairs inside the monument and the tree of life was at the top as you came out into the light and you climbed toward it and there were tears in your eyes and it sounds stupid but you were real fucked in the head and it meant a lot at the time and, no. I said we weren't doing this.

Scrolling Facebook Memes Waiting for the Paediatrician

Elisabeth Ingram Wallace, winner, 2020 The Forge Literary Magazine Flash Competition

Aoccdrnig to rscheearch at Cmabrigde Uinervtisy it deosn't mttaer in waht oredr the ltteers in a word are, the olny ipromoatnt tihng is that the frist and lsat ltteers be at the rghit pclae. The rset can be a toatl mses, yuo can sitll raed it wouthit porbelm. Tihs is bcuseae the huamn mnid does not raed every lteter by istlef, but the wrod as a wlohe.

The Dcotors take me into a pink room of folral 1970's wllapepar, a samll plasitc plnat and a box of tssiues on the tbale, and tell me "Baby" is not OK.

"Baby" is yuo, and I'm "Dad"-- myabe tehy can't rembemer our nmaes, myabe this is infantsiliing-hopsital-mandetad Dcotor-spaek—but eethir way, I like it.

  I am a "Dad." Yuor Dad.

  A Dcotor spaeks.

  "Baby has bad cennoctions, like brkoen wriing or msifirings."

"The organs mgiht fail," one says, and I thnik of big pink church noises.

"We are monitirong his heart."

"In a months' time we'll konw more."

I thnik of the moon getting thinner and thinner.

Can he haer me sing to him, talk to him? How mcuh he can see?

"We msut wait and see."

"We can't talk in years."

Correct, I reply. We must talk in ineadquate words.

"OK," the Dcotor says.

"We'll take one day at a time."

This particular Dcotor wishes he was dozing in his office driinkng pond-tempareture Nescafe, listineng to the clock tick-tock towards home time, raeding his favuorite book, "70 Inane Clichés for Heartbroken Parents."

Plaese, can I just take my son home? I say.

"No. His organs will fail," they reply. Big pink church noises. I look at the walls.

I see thnigs, like Sundays, melting.

"It's all up in the air," the Dcotor says.

What yaer is it in here? I say.

I point at the wllpaaper.

These flewors are 1974, the piasley is a rael 1979 vibe. Tihs room is a wlohe decade.

Their chiars scrik-skrack back, whack to the walls; they look over my shuolders thruogh the doors, over my haed--anywehre but at me.

They hover like inscets in pollen.

"Look."

"We'll wiat and see."

"We'll keep a clsoe eye on him."

They talk at ecah other in language of eyeballs.

The pink walls are bubble-gum stcuk in my hair, Hubba-Bubba days, cherry-pop nihgts; I had 70's wallpaper back then, psychdeelic pink flower-power on my 80's bderoom walls; pink, raw as sunburn, peeilng shoulders, sacchirane strawberry yoghurts, forever Sundays; early to bed; it's still light outside and the TV is always on. My parents are both alive in this memory.

Mum and Dad, both, downstairs, cooking kidneys with onion, Bisto, Smash; their big box TV playing chat-show-voices big-brassy-music, canned luaghter, Mums fresh luaghter on top, Dads own luagh so deep yuo could tuck yuorself into it, slip right under a ha ha ha ha ha ha ha applause.

It makes me cry to think of Mum and Dad.

WE CAN TALK AGIAN LATER the Dcotors say.

WE CAN SEE THIS IS A DFFIICULT TIME FOR YUO.

I see things, behind the Dcotors. Flewors arrengad like women in a wedding picture, pink-orange-red lips fading to nicotine-yollew, snaps in an album—old coluors now, but we grew up iinsde them. Chucrh halls, muffled coughs. Cold metal handles on oak veneer. Our Father who art in Heaven, sore thraots, a toddler cry. My M&S black nylon tie. Dust to dust. Wet triangles, egg sandwiches.

Baby.

Next door in yuor ward cot, yuo are sleeping strong and cool like the basement of a Georgian museum cafe with a cffoee machine growling inside it; that ten-week-old snow-fall afternoon when yuo were just a haertbeat and we drank ginger beer that fizzzzzzzzzzzzed and we shared ginger cake too, until my thorax burned due-date-July-heatwaves and yuor Mum stopped wanting to puke, and we raed about baby Mozart.

Listen, Kid, even *sound* can make a brain strnoger, do yuo know that? Music, words, my memoreis are a ttoal mess but yuo've got to listen aruond the gaps and feel the noise burn, to raed a wlohe life.

 I am the hum yuo can hear.

 The hot hand tapping on yuor small fat belly, monitoring yuor heart.

 Yuo are running—running in yuor sleep—yuor too little legs twitch twitch twitch and sometimes yuo ORF bark a bubble-bark like my old dog Daisy did in her dreams, and I know yuo are chasing sparrows in yuor head, like Daisy did, but the sparrows in yuor head are thin, silver-glitches falling out the trees, dead drops, each time yuor heart monitor stops. Someone is cooking garlic in a pan in the Mexican food van beside Paediatrics and yuor toy cat purrs, and I laugh at your little legs, sprint sprinting nowhere, or somewhere. Hunt the ducks, hunt the sky, bark ORF at the moon. It's all up in the air.

Sea Change

Sharon Telfer, winner, 2016 Hysteria Flash Fiction Competition

My heart sank.

I watched it go. It fought hard to keep afloat. I took my boathook, knocked back its jellyfish pulses. I had to make sure. Cracked, it bubbled silver as it dropped, an aspirin fizz then one toxic gulp like mercury breaking from a thermometer. It stopped struggling after that, twisted, turned in the tug of the tide, spiralling slowly down into the deep dark.

I watched until I could see it no more.

My mother warned me. You never know when you might want it back. To shut her up, I marked it by the harbour buoy. I knew I wouldn't need it again. I crossed off years well enough without it, the sea coming in, going out, working, eating, sleeping. Except on stormy nights. The wild clamour of the buoy bell woke me then. I'd hug the pillow over my ears and curse my mother.

But she was right. Of course.

There you were, one day, end of the pier, leaning into the wind like a figurehead. For the first time since I drowned my heart, I licked my roughened, seaside lips and tasted salt.

That night I rowed out and let down my net. I threw back the crabs and the mackerel, rubbed off the barnacle crust by the light of the moon. My pearlescent heart shone, strange, hard, beautiful.

I bent my back to the oars and headed for land, heart thumping like a fresh caught fish.

Search History

Iain Rowan, winner, 2012 Flashbang Crime Flash Fiction Contest

internet dating

what to wear on a first date

seduction techniques

Italian restaurants

Italian restaurants, happy hour special offers

love at first sight is it real?

how soon is too soon to propose?

engagement rings

engagement rings platinum

engagement rings platinum interest free credit

engagement rings gold

how not to be overbearing in relationship

WEDDING VENUES

what does it mean partner want space

is there a conference at the Park Hotel on Tuesday

ten signs your partner is seeing someone else

how trace call hung up no answer

anger management tips online

how I can recover deleted texts from iPhone?

strategies to keep temper

keylogger for windows how do I

how to keep calm

twenty ways to keep your cool

best place to hide GPS in car

anger management

confront partner suspect cheating what say

confront partner suspect cheating how keep temper

anger management

anger management

anger management

anger management

anger management

woodchipper hire

carpet cleaning services

industrial bleach

plastic sheeting

best prices sell gold engagement ring

internet dating.

Self/Less

Electra Rhodes, winner, 2021 Federation of Scottish Writers Flash Competition

I.

It starts with a single word. Dropped.
Misplaced.

Simply a_s_nt.

Like a crossword missing some letters.

But it's fine.

It is just *a* word. Just one.

[John slits open the post. I watch as the envelope bleeds under his nibbling thimbling fumbles. It is an important letter which says I have won an award for a lifetime of distinguished service to literature. John is happy. I think I know what this means.
I am gracious in my acceptance.]

But then it becomes more than   word. Though it is
                                only   word at _ time.

And there are enough words,   glorious majestic
expression after another that the absence of   might
be leapt over by the eye.

            [And no   really notices. Or so it seems.]

                        II.

It is a swathe.
            A crop.
                        A panoply.
                                    A collation.
                                                A tumble.

And other things begin to go…?!
Punctuation—What is : and why is she not crying, like
her sister on the keyboard ; ;

   [I write an essay about the death of punctuation and the
                                desolation of her family.

It wins an award for satire.
I don't collect the prize.]

[John tells me this was a dream. Or a misremembering. No essay. No prize. I hope he is telling me the truth.]

III.

It isn't only words. Or punctuation. It is plot. And character. And the technical foibles that made the words sing. Like a conductor. Words dancing in the air. Notes, suspended. The music of the spheres. The everything. The all. The all. The sea. The

[John finds me crying in the garden. I tell him Me has taken the words and buried them in the flowerbeds. That I must find them. He is kind. Tells me if they are seeds they will bloom.

From the bedroom window I look out over the moonlit garden and see it is now an impenetrable jungle of story. Eyes cry.

In the morning the flowers are gone.]

IV.

Meaning. Meaning. Meaning. Self. Self. Self. Love.

[In a brush of lucidity where I paint words across the air with ease I tell John that I can see the irony in losing my *self* when that is what has exercised me for so long. He reminds me I am happy in myself. I am not sure what this means.]

The paint runs. Away. Colours washed out by rain sweat tears semen sea. The sea. The sea.

V.

I still have words though they fit in edgeways.

I still have words though they fit.

[I still have words though.]

I still have.

Still.

VI.

[I think, 'This is what it means to be buried alive'.]

VII.

There is sky. And sea.   home. And darkness   stars.

And

And

                                                        [   ]

And

                  Clay

                                      Lumped

              Misshapen

                                    [I am kilned.]

Glazed

All at sea.

                        [Words dissolving. Like]

                  You.

            Love.

                             [ ]

                  Me.

[There is no Me. But. The self, truly *selfing*, means, I am free]

The self and the sea. The self and the sea. The self and sea.

              A drowning.

              And

                              [me.]

Silent Space

Jane Roberts, winner, 2013 Writers & Artists Flash Fiction Competition

His parents argue. Ad infinitum. Preoccupied, they don't notice the alteration in their son after he browses a science website in the public library, that comforting place immersed in silence away from the uncertain world of trying to match distorted noises with the right people or machines.

He can't always hear them arguing. Clouded expressions, staccato movements are enough to gauge the mood. Coffee mugs obscure lips; wine glasses share partially-transparent secrets; the signs they make with their fingers not quite part of his official language. Something has to change. But his words queue up in the limbo between thought and voice; writing emerges confused.

He finds everything in the local pound shop—black, blue, white, silver paint, and tin foil. Phosphorous stars now glow on the ceiling, planets dot his navy duvet, and spaceship silver pimps the furniture.

When they notice his absence, he can see their arguing stops upon entering his bedroom—their mouths exposing Merlot-dyed tongues suspended like stomped-out leather shoe soles.

    Now they hear the same thing, all three of them a mute constellation amongst the tin foil stars in his silent space.

Sins of the Heart
ROMANS Chapter 1 verse 29
Kit de Waal, winner, 2014 Bridport Flash Fiction Prize

She needs bread.

"I'll be five minutes," she sings and her heartbeat drums her across the road, around the corner, down the hill. She wears slippers and carries a tea towel, clean, unused. She has neighbours, her journey needs the props of innocence. But he is not there tending his front garden. His neat and slender house is shadowy and locked.

"We need milk," she chimes, and fastens her baby in the pushchair as restraint. She sees him waiting and his smile is worth her shame.

One Sunday the minister points to close print on rice paper and speaks of sins imagined, words unsaid. He traces footsteps from her husband's bed all the way across the road, around the corner, down the hill and she has weeks to wait before God looks away.

She has a list and calls us inside.

"Do we have to?"

"Yes, you have to," she mutters and foists cold coins in my sister's hand. We cross the road, around the corner, down the hill. A man as tall as my father leans on an open gate like he knows us. Dark soil escapes from his trowel.

We carry her bag home one handle each, potatoes, flour, unnecessary things and, as we pass, he tips his hat and says hello. He has sweets, dusty, pink and everlasting.

"Did you see anyone?'" she asks.

We spill her change and our adventure on the kitchen table and she slips away.

"Forgot the sugar," she whispers, "forgot the eggs."

Snow Crow

Doug Ramspeck, winner, Bath Flash Fiction Award, October 2021

And the days were made of auguries. And the cricket calls arrived disembodied from the field. And a dead mole lay on its back by the garage, gathering its thin blanket of ants. And wasps hummed outside the boy's window like primitive wraiths. And one morning, he found a dead crow in the woods and carried it back to the house, hiding it at the back of his closet like a reliquary. And sometimes he imagined the creature calling to him in the night, calling to him in his dreams, and the boy would rise, pull the string for the closet light, and open the cardboard box. And there was the crow: its dark wings motionless, its dark and lacquered eyes gazing up at him. And sometimes in the mornings, the boy stepped into the backyard and gazed at the sun with its raw, sepulchral eye. And at breakfast, now and then, he asked about his father. And his mother would cross her arms over her chest or set his plate so forcefully on the table that the boy would look away. And some afternoons, he sat in his closet and imagined the crow lifting itself on the dark oars of its wings, rowing high above the trees. Or the boy imagined a crow call fissuring the air, a crow call that was both corporeal and incorporeal at once. And the smell in the boy's closet was like something secretive congealing on the surface of a pond. And on the evening when a first light snow of the season came dropping toward the land, the boy carried the crow back into the woods and tossed it as high as he could manage into the air.

Sometimes There's Compassion in a Punch

Peter Burns, winner, Flash 500 Competition, Nov 2020

When Da booked our first holiday, a weekend in a caravan in St. Andrews, Ma wept.

Sometimes people cry without being hurt.

It took three hours, two trains, and one bus to get there. Da bought cans of beer on the last train. Ma tutted about the price, but kept on smiling.

Sometimes it's better not knowing the course ahead.

Da was drunk when we arrived at the caravan. Picking up Ma, he carried her through the door. Ma said it was fifteen years too late, but, still, better late than never. Da wasn't angry when he put her down.

Sometimes surprises swell up so fast you're almost swept away.

There was only one bedroom. The couch in the living-room pulled out to become a mattress. They said I could sleep there and watch telly until the national anthem came on. But Da was snoring by nine o'clock and Ma nodded for me to come into bed beside her.

Sometimes it might seem calm, but it's still there, circling under the surface.

We went to the beach, next day. Me and Ma paddled in the sea, splashing its cold saltiness into each other's faces. Ma's cheeks reddened and a tinge of blue struck through her lips, yet Da was sleeping far behind us.

Sometimes good things become memories too.

At a wee shop on the way home, Da bought me and Ma an ice-cream. A plastic bag filled with cans of beer swung from his wrist. We're all happy now, he said. Ma smiled, shivers streaking her bare legs.

Sometimes a person's body tells more truth than their face ever could.

The couch in the caravan was C shaped. Da lay across one side, nearest the telly, and me and Ma sat across from him. The middle part was no man's land.

Sometimes fighting can be silent and small.

Last evening of the holiday, Da took us with him to the pub. Ma said in fifteen years that was another new thing. We sat at a table outside, looking over a cliff to the sea. We had fish and chips and I was allowed as much ginger as I wanted. Ma had a glass of wine, but it was nowhere near Christmas. Da drank beer like a drowning man needing air. The sky was a scarlet and purple bruise on our way home, Da staggering far behind us. Just before the caravan park a rabbit lay at the side of the road, twitching and bleeding. Ma covered her mouth, clasped her stomach. Da came and bent down, stroked it with one hand, made a fist with the other. Ma pushed me behind her. But I wanted to see. I wanted to see what had slowed Da's breathing, what had furrowed his brow, what had heaved his shoulders up before they curled downwards like a wave.

Sometimes there's compassion in a punch.

Teavarran

Louise J Jones (originally published under Louise Swingler), winner, 2019 Fish Flash Fiction Prize

She can never believe how bright the gorse is, laid in great yellow arcs across the land. She breathes its coconut tang as she walks up the lane.

She can hear the gurgling veins of Scotland in the beck that runs in the ditch beside her. It's twelve degrees here, cool after London's twenty-four. The relief of it is a sensual chiding. She fits well here. Where does Thomas fit, though? You know I don't do "green", he says, whenever she asks him to come home with her.

She had wanted to come at Christmas, and in March.

A quad bike roars and she steps aside. Clumps of dock leaves are already growing back on the roughly-cropped verge. The one time he came, Thomas said these lanes ruined his suspension. He didn't seem to realise how victorious this strip of tarmac is, checking the unstoppable push of the forest. But she knows it is but a temporary occupation. She enjoys this challenge to mankind's arrogance.

Her father's Highland cattle, flank deep, munch steadily through yellow rattle and buttercups. Two auburn calves are submerged like islands in an inland ocean of green, beige, purple, yellow. They raise their snubby noses, eyeing her. She thinks of Thomas, eyeing her as she left him at Luton Airport.

She looks across to the hills and the peaks behind them. The sky is a dull pearl, flat and quiet, and the morning mist has frozen into a row of frail tufts along the valley bottom, as if a steam train had recently departed.

She turns and stares into the calf's swimming eyes, daring him.

"If you don't move before I blink, I'll stay."

Tick. Tock.

Her eyes begin to water. The calf remains still. Like a painting that Thomas can't climb into. She blinks.

Ten Months with Octopus

Angela Readman, winner, 2019 New Flash Fiction Review Anton Chekhov Prize

1. *Even when severed from the body the limbs of an octopus can function on their own.* I clean outside the tanks at Sea Land and catch the display, rubber squidgy screaming over wet glass. The couple nearby have pink streaks in their hair like they shared something last night. They snap a photo and kiss still clutching their phones.

2. The street I had to move to has a kid who keeps dragging an inflatable squid across the lawn. It's sunny and his parents are estranged. When his father collects him, his mother picks lint off his shirt and withdraws fast. Standing by the paddling pool, she doesn't wave at the VW pulling away. Her hands behind her back clasp her elbows.

3. The oranges are so cheap all July the market sells them in nets. I carry some home, fruit squeezing through mesh, juice bleeding like macerated

sunshine on my legs. The fruit bowl got smashed, I forgot that. I lay the oranges out like a clock on the table and picture someone peeling one long strip of lingering rind.

4. Houdini the Octopus has left the building. They imagine he squeezed through a drain & will find himself at the ocean like a surfer who thinks he left his keys in the door. I say this aloud, turning towards the cushion as if it may find this funny. I switch a programme about wallpaper to something about homeowners and self-defence.

5. I find a shirt one Friday and freeze. It's fluff flecked, squeezed into a ball behind the cushions. I should have left the couch in the old flat. Later, I find a leather belt poking out like a tongue. I lay the pair out and sit beside them when I answer the phone. My sister's pregnant again and worried about her blood pressure. I tell her everything will be fine, fiddling with the belt, winding it around my ankle until my foot turns blue.

6. Only losers spend Halloween as themselves. I put on a sequinned skirt and slit it to the hip for a party at work. If pushed, I'll say I'm a mermaid. No one asks. Everyone's a sea creature of some description, even the IT guys. I get stuck talking to one dressed as an office worker, other than for a rubber fish mask he pulls out of his pocket occasionally as evidence he tried. I'm pretty, for someone with such a sad face, he claims. He smiles. I tell him to put the fish mask on again.

7. I shag him, though I refuse to move on from shit. I drag memories around everywhere and crouch under them for minutes at a time. There's a chance this makes me seem enigmatic. We've just seen The Shape of Water and, curled on the couch, somehow my socked feet have squirmed their way under IT guy's legs, found their hot weight. During, he holds my left breast. Just one like he daren't want too much. I look at him and wish he still had the fish mask. He asks what I'm thinking. I inform him an octopus has three hearts.

8. I agree to see him on Christmas Eve to exchange gifts. It's too soon for much. I get him a Manatea to perch on his cup making fruit infusions with its tail. It looks like a walrus who had its teeth smashed in while everyone was in bed. Honestly, I only like the name, a manatee united with tea. There should be more words that include things, like widow- a combo of marriage and death. There's no equivalent for girlfriends. Girls called Diedra write died every day. There's no meaning for the rest of their name.

9. I let Fishface stay over in January. During the night, my legs weave through his, a sleeping arm drapes him like bindweed. He binds back, we drift into wakefulness like that, intertwined. I start a fight over breakfast about politics, global warming, bacon. The words are black ink squirting the air. In the cloud they leave behind, I can scuttle away, slam a door, wrap that stinking shirt I found in the couch around me and breathe.

10. It's been a while, but he calls, apologies for his opinions on fishing rights, poached eggs, and not getting dressed as soon as he's awake. I peer through the door, open a crack and look at him—a slither of dork in black cords and a Houdini shirt. He's holding out a plant growing from a sea urchin. For my bathroom, it looks kind of bare. It needs no water, he claims, only air. I light a cigarette and tell him I'll probably kill it anyway. It will keel over without me doing a thing. His morning breath alone could do it, I say, my fingers on the lock close the space between us before they open the chain.

The Button Wife

Dara Yen Elerath, winner, Bath Flash Fiction Award, June 2021

The button wife bends her body across the bed, but the cloth husband is not interested in touching her. Instead, he phones the burlap wife. He likes the way her coarse skin brushes against his body. At night, the button wife cries, recalling how her husband used to clutch the dark thread of her hair. She knows the burlap wife's curls scratch him in the fashion he prefers. The cloth husband has a passion for roughness, but the button wife, woven from cotton, has only been soft and yielding. One evening, she decides to scour the buttons of her eyes with steel wool; she hopes her husband will love her again. Soon, they are scuffed and cracked. When her husband comes back he looks at her with anger. *You have ruined your eyes*, he says, *how can I look at you now?* Later, gazing in a hand mirror, she notes she is no longer beautiful. She lifts a pair of scissors and snips the strings that knot the buttons to her face. Then she can no longer weep; then she can no longer see her husband leave the house each evening. She irons the hem of her dress in darkness. She waits to hear the sound of his car speeding down plastic blacktop. She dreams of the burlap wife's hair cutting her skin the way it cuts her husband's. Sometimes, she pricks her arm with a darning needle to feel. The red thread that unspools from her body is long as a dog leash. She wonders then if she is a dog. She hopes the cloth husband will walk her when he returns. She resolves then to wag her tail in greeting. She resolves then to sleep at his feet.

The Cinders of 2021

Kevin Cheeseman, winner, Writers Forum 500 Words Contest, Jan 2022

Scene: The Royal Ball. Prince Charming and his aide, Dandini, are surveying the packed ballroom.

Prince: Ah, the Royal Ball! Isn't it marvellous, Dandini?

Dandini: It's a marvel we're even holding it, what with a pandemic raging across the land and the decree against having parties.

Prince: Oh, does that rule apply to us?

Dandini (*rolls his eyes*): Don't worry, sire. We'll just say it's a work meeting.

Prince: Good plan, Dandini! And it's fair enough, actually. I mean, if this isn't a Royal Prince's job, what is?

Dandini (*aside*): Good question…

Prince: Look, there's Baron Hardup. He really is the most awful man. How on earth did he get to be a Baron?

Dandini: The King ennobled him, sire. For services rendered.

Prince: Really? What sort of services?

Dandini: The £3 million pound donation sort. He's not as poor as he tells the taxman, you know.

Prince: I see he's brought daughters, Teresa and Tracey
Dandini: Ah, the infamous Tess and Trace. (*Aside*) Very expensive and utterly useless.
Prince: They're the only guests wearing face masks. That's very responsible of them, isn't it?
Dandini: Not really. I told the doorman not to let them in without masks on. I didn't want their ugly mugs scaring everyone.

(*At the side, Cinderella, preparing to enter, speaks with Fairy Godmother*)

Cinderella: Thanks for everything, Fairy Godmother: the makeover, the gown, the glass slippers. That carriage you magicked up was a-ma-zing, darling—although it was a bit cramped inside.
Fairy Godmother: It's made from a pumpkin—it was bound to be a squash. Just remember, you must leave by midnight or the spell will be broken. Look out, Prince Charming is coming over—good luck!
Prince: Sweet mistress, your beauty astounds me—why have I never seen you before? Have you been in quarantine?

Cinderella: Social isolation, more like. Eighteen flipping years of it.
Prince: But why so long?
Cinderella: Basically, because of a patriarchal, plutocratic system that tolerates nepotism, perpetuates the impoverishment of the proletariat, and subjugates women.
Prince: Come again?
Cinderella: Never mind. Are you going to ask me to dance or what?

They dance and dance, but the hands on the clock begin to race. Cinderella notices it is nearly midnight and runs off in panic.

Prince: Help me, Dandini—that beautiful girl has disappeared and I don't even know her name. The only clue she left is this glass slipper. How will I ever find her?
Dandini: Fear not, sire. We will scour the land performing LFTs on all young women.
Prince: LFTs?
Dandini: Lost Footwear Tests. Whoever the slipper fits will be your mystery girl.

Prince: That's ingenious, Dandini. Although, you know that a positive LFT has to be confirmed by PCR.

Dandini: PCR?

Prince: Prince Charming's Reaction. I'll look in her eyes and if my heart starts to pound, she's the one.

Dandini: (*aside*) Good to see he's following the science.

Prince: Come, Dandini! We leave at dawn!

[END]

The Eight Year Hope of Us (as seen on TV)
Lucy Goldring, winner, Lunate Journal Flash Competition, July 2020

1996

The night before you go, we choke on our wine watching Jarvis Cocker waft farts at Wacko Jacko. By the time we stop laughing our thighs have fused in the sofa sag. You get up to refill the crisps. We retreat to our respective ends. As your warmth leaves my body, I realise I love you.

1998

You're back from Japan. We're flinging our arms around at a petulant Beckham—the entire pub is. There's no fusion this time; just unreadable glances through eye-stinging smoke and lager fumes. Over the uproar, I hear you've met someone there: a Londoner. I'm prostrate on the pitch, kicking life hard (in the calf).

2000

To get addicted to reality TV, simply view once for research purposes. Big Brother fills cracks in my life, effaces my summer. It frees my brain to wonder about newly single you. At the ads, I flick over to MTV. Gawking at Kylie's revolving golden orbs, I worry for us both.

2002

I'm bewitched as Ricky Gervais transforms cringe into art. *Are you watching this??* I want to text—but it's not my turn. Our last fortnightly exchange ended with an "*x*". The value of *x* is *hope*. It peeps from its hiding space like a nervous rescue pet.

2004

Your text says "passing through". I calculate the thirty-mile diversion and smile.

You in my porch flips me sideways. We fail at small talk, inanities colliding like impatient door users. I stick on the box, toes unclenching, and gesture to the sofa.

Kelly Holmes is prepping for the 800 metres. She powers through on the final bend to take Gold. We jump up into a clumsy high-five.

Just biding her time you say; your hand warm on my shoulder, my hope a fluff-ball bouncing round the room.

The First Man on the Moon
Rosie Garland, winner, Lunate Journal 500 Competition, May 2020

Upon landing, Johannes Kepler looks back at Earth, a blue-green ball tossed high in lunar sky. He makes the grunt of satisfaction known to his most intimate friends, dips quill and writes: *one can only experience such homesick affection when one admires a beloved object from afar.*

His first steps stagger. Despite the wine steeped in opium, the damp sponges squeezed into his nostrils, he cannot shake off queasiness. Four hours in the arms of demons is the most enervating method of transportation imaginable, more exhausting than a haycart bounced over rocks.

He fans his cheek, scorching beneath a sun that seems so much closer than on Earth. On his return, he will advertise the attractions of this kingdom. Let Spain and France squabble over the Americas. Before him stretches the pinnacle and prize of new-found lands.

When selecting colonists, neither desk-bound men nor dandies deserve such high adventure. Sailors, perhaps; men accustomed to defying the ocean's titanic pressures. He pauses, ink dripping onto his shoe.

No. Far better to send old women to break the ground of these grey hills. Unruly crones dried-out from riding goats and broom-handles, skilled in the throwing-off of Europe's heavy air. If they can cover the wide face of a continent in the wink of one night's eye, travelling to the Moon will be a trifle. Besides, they are accustomed to congress with devils, so will mate readily with Moon-men. Their offspring shall build mansions suited to men of high estate.

He consults his pocket watch. Lights the bonfire at the hour arranged, so that his wife knows to prepare the goose and parsnips in readiness for his return. He grits his teeth, waits for angels.

The Grand Finale

Tim Craig, winner, 2018 Bridport Flash Fiction Prize

Even by his own high standards, The Great Fantoni's world tour had been a triumph. The crowds had turned out in their thousands to welcome him wherever he went and the newspaper reviews had proclaimed the show his best yet.

When the magician finally arrived home, he handed his coat and jacket to his wife and announced that he would be going straight to bed.

Mrs Great Fantoni wished her husband a good night and, although she was tired herself, said that she would unpack his things for him before retiring.

After he had gone up, she dragged his large, monogrammed trunk down the hallway and into the sitting room. There, she undid the gold clasps, lifted the heavy lid, and took out a hinged leather portmanteau.

From this, she removed a vintage suitcase, which she noted still bore the faded destination label from their honeymoon. Inside the suitcase was a hand-tooled crocodile skin valise, which, in turn, held an old canvas rucksack.

Scrunched up in the rucksack was a blue sports holdall, from which she pulled a plastic supermarket bag containing her husband's cheap floral wash bag.

She unzipped the wash bag and took out his orange plastic toothbrush holder. She popped this open to discover an empty foil condom packet from which, with a flourish—and the sound of triumphant applause ringing in her ears—she extracted the children, the house and half the money.

The Hand That Wields the Priest
Emily Devane, winner, Bath Flash Fiction Award, Feb 2017

That evening, the fish left a strange taste in my mouth.

We'd gone together, Dad in his waxed jacket and waders, me in my parka and wellies. Flies hovered above the river, orange-tinged in the afternoon sun. He fastened together his rod and opened his box: flies lined up like soldiers on parade. "We'll try the March Brown," he said, affixing one to the line.

I spied the metal hook; it glinted between his fingers.

"Can you see him?" he pointed to a pool of slow-moving water. "There," he said and I followed his finger to a set of tiny ripples where, seconds ago, a mouth had snapped.

While I sat on a long-rotten stump, he waded in. Shoulders stretched back then thrown forward, he cast the fly towards the pool to dance across the water's surface. He held his body still a while, then cast again. Patience is required, he whispered. When I tried to speak, to ask if the fish had gone, he shushed me. A glimmer of something, more ripples.

The rod bent—and then jerked to and fro. Dad reeled him in, the fish fighting all the while to shake off the metal hook. On land, he thrashed and gasped for breath—the gills, Dad indicated with his fingertips.

One shiny eye gazed up from the bag. With his hand, the same one he used to stroke my head at night, Dad gave a firm whack with his metal priest. The thrashing stopped.

A priest, I wondered. Was that to save its soul?

Dad held the fish across his hands for me to see the tiny teeth that took the bite, the shimmering belly.

"Would you look at that," he said.

That night, his hand felt different on my head.

The Haunted Pan

Phil Olsen, winner, 2017 Northern Short Story Festival Flash Fiction Slam

"So, have you had any paranormal experiences in this house?"

"Nope, I've not heard a peep from the ghosts in the three years I've lived here. I do have a haunted pan though."

"A haunted pan?"

"Yeah, it's a glass pan that was here when I moved in. I clean it after use and it comes up sparkling, completely clear. But then it dries filthy."

"Hmm, perhaps that is more to do with your cleaning abilities than any cuisine spectres?"

"I know what you're thinking…"

"Of course you know what I'm thinking, I just told you what I'm thinking. I'm thinking your domestic skills leave a lot to be desired."

"But wait, there's more. Every time I cook food in the pan, it comes out as a fancy Victorian meal with all the trimmings. No matter what I cook. I usually only throw together a simple spag bol, but when I pour it out of the glass pan I get pheasant with all kinds of trimmings. Plus, when I'm done eating the pan's olden days' meal, my stomach can walk through walls."

"Your stomach can?"

"Yup."

"Just your stomach?"

"Yeah, that's the snag. I can jut my belly out and press it through any door or wall, but the rest of me stays solid and gets blocked. So I've experimented with it a little and I've tried occasionally pouring the food all over me. Rubbing it in my hair, you know? I had it all planned out…I had a mouthful of unswallowed guinea fowl, two fists of sage & onion stuffing, and my cardigan pockets were loaded with carrot & parsnip mash."

"No joy though?"

"The opposite of joy. I'd taken a bit of a run up…You can probably make out where I hit the wall… Just doesn't come clean. Or rather it does wipe clean quite easily, but then it dries dirty again."

"Like the pan."

"Exactly like the pan. It's a shame really, 'cause I would have only ever used the power it gave me for good, you know?"

"There'd be quite a lot of preparation involved

before you could go to the rescue of someone who'd, say, locked themselves out of their flat though, wouldn't there? I mean with the whole having to cook a meal and then all the subsequent distributing of the food about your person...They could probably get a locksmith out in less time."

"Hey, maybe that's it! Maybe the food has to still be piping hot throughout when it comes into contact with the wall. Maybe I'm just taking too long..."

"And all these clothes piled on the table and the Welsh dresser...Looks like you've attempted it a few times. I take it the food washes clean out, but then comes back encrusted into the fabric when the clothes dry?"

"Pretty much...Say...You guys aren't really from *Most Haunted*, are you?"

"No, Mr Sammons, we're not really from *Most Haunted*. We're from Social Services."

"Yeah well, fuck you, you fuckers, I'm gonna run through that wall right now and then you'll see..."

"Shall I put the hob on for you?"

"It probably won't work in front of you...The Victorian meal thing, I mean."

"No, Mr Sammons, I imagine it probably won't."

The Letter from the Home Office
Gail Anderson, winner, 2022 Edinburgh Award for Flash Fiction

It spins up on a thermal, fluttering in a sparrow-brown envelope (second class) and when she reaches to catch it, her hot-air balloon lurches. Eleven years aloft in a brittle basket of willow, a moth-wing billow overhead. A hailstorm might send her plummeting, a hurricane spiralling stratospheric. She longs to land—but she is not allowed. When gravity pulls, she feeds the hungry burner forms and proofs, fistfuls of cash, until the firebox burns bright. It's hard work, staying up—but the view is striking. Green quilts hemmed in hawthorn, ruched with oak and ash. A molecule of sheepdog moves a puddle of milk between meadows. She counts hours on a clock of standing stones. From this height history's hard edges are buried. Children wave as she floats overhead. Adults squint up, shielding their eyes. "Are you on holiday?" "When do you go home?" Their tinny voices fizz her ether. There are days she wishes for the storm that would blow her far away from this place. But now, sliding her thumb under the brown paper flap, reading the words inside, the seams of her rainbow silk start to shred. Down she goes: through clouds, past radio towers, pigeons dodging. Past bored office-block faces, tumbling through horn-blasting, flag-waving air, the street rushing to meet her in a stink of bins and wet and diesel. Belonging here, she knows, will be a new kind of distance. This is the price of the ground beneath her feet.

The Lighthouse Project
Vanessa Gebbie, winner, 2006 Small Wonder Festival Flash Slam

Max watched the boy through the telescope for over an hour. Thanks to some collusion between evening sunlight and prisms the boy's skin looked like mercury under liquid honey. It poured through the tamarisk shadows, breached the old stone walls, ran up to the top of the lighthouse, where it seeped out of the eyepiece and ran, warm, down Max's chest.

Max had seen the boy slamming the door of a white van parked on the headland, walking away, flinging words over thin shoulders, hiding, until the van drove off in a spit of gravel, a thick-fingered V sign waving out of the window.

Finally, the boy came to the lighthouse. "Can I use your phone?" he said

Max leaned against the door frame. "Sure. Need the phone book?"

"Nah. Ringing my stepdad's mobile, in the caravan." He brushed past Max, picked up the phone. "Thanks." He paused. "You live here?" he said, looking at the cheap wardrobe, the bed against the wall, the open suitcase, paperbacks. The door to the spiral staircase, ajar.

"No. Holiday."

"You sell books?"

Max smiled. "No. Read them."

"Huh. You a teacher or something?"

Max stopped smiling. "I was."

"Oh, right." The boy dialled, then, "His phone's off. Nemmind. I'll walk." His shoulders relaxed.

Max breathed deeply. "It's getting dark." He could walk down the track behind the boy, past the sign that said *Private, Lighthouse closed to the public,* watching the tendons behind the boy's knees.

The boy hesitated. "You could help me do a project on lighthouses," he said.

The boy stood under the huge Victorian glass prisms which striped his face, his shoulders, with dying sunlight. He could have been looking in at Max through bars.

He moved. Put one hand up to the telescope. "What do you watch?" Then he answered himself. "Birds. I was down there, wasn't I?"

"Were you?" said Max, remembering the boy's trainers skittering among the tamarisk roots like dirty white mice.

The boy, on tiptoe, squinted into the eyepiece. "Do you watch those white birds on the cliff, up on the ledges?"

His eyelashes were dark. There were tiny hairs on his forearms. Every hair had a minute shadow. Max shut his eyes. The boy stayed imprinted on his retina like a sepia photograph, a small jungle animal, taut, ready to run.

But he was still talking. "Why don't those birds fall off the ledges when they're asleep?" A tooth caught on his lip. The tip of his tongue flicked out, bright with spittle.

Max held on to the mahogany surround that enclosed the prisms like a dark fist. "Things are what they are," he said. "Seabirds fly, even in their sleep."

The boy turned to look at him. "Does this lighthouse still work?"

"It would. All it needs is someone to throw the switch." Max looked out at the horizon, a bright smouldering fuse where the sun was soundlessly setting the sea on fire.

The Long Wet Grass

Seamus Scanlon, winner, 2011 Fish Flash Fiction Prize

The resonance of tires against the wet road is a mantra, strong and steady. The wipers slough rain away in slow rhythmic arcs into the surrounding blackness. The rain falls slow and steady, then gusting, reminding me of Galway when I was a child where Atlantic winds flung broken fronds of seaweed onto the Prom during high tide. Before the death harmony of Belfast seduced me.

The wind keeps trying to tailgate us. But we keep sailing. The slick black asphalt sings on beneath us. We slow and turn onto a dirt road, the clean rhythm now broken, high beams tracing tall reeds edging against the road, moving rhythmically back and forth with the wind. No lights now from oncoming cars.

We stop at a clearing. I open the door, the driver looks back at me. The rain on my face is soothing. The pungent petrol fumes comfort me. The moon lies hidden behind black heavy clouds. I unlock the trunk.

You can barely stand after lying curled up for hours. After a while you can stand straight. I take the tape from your mouth. You breathe in the fresh air. You breathe in the fumes. You watch me. You don't beg. You don't cry. You are brave.

I hold your arm and lead you away from the roadway, into a field, away from the car, from the others. The gun in my hand pointed at the ground. I stop. I kiss your cheek. I raise the gun. I shoot you twice high in the temple. The coronas of light anoint you. You fall. The rain rushes to wipe the blood off. I fire shots into the air. The ejected shells skip away.

I walk back to the car and leave you there lying in the long wet grass.

The Most Fascinating Woman in the World

Andrew Boulton, winner, Cranked Anvil Magazine Flash Fiction Contest, Feb 2021

When it became clear she truly was the most fascinating woman in the world, everybody wanted to be near her. And, because she genuinely was a fascinating woman, and hadn't simply been mistaken for one, she could think of nothing worse to be than fascinating.

At first, it was intrusive but never especially dangerous. People would wait outside her fascinating apartment and trail her through the streets to whichever fascinating place she was going. Such was the fascination with what she bought, read and ate, that she could no longer do any of these things without an audience pressed hungrily up against the glass, fogging the windows of her favourite shops and cafes with admiring breath. She even tried going to the least fascinating places she could think of, eating bland food and reading awful books, but all this did was make everybody fascinated with vulgar things, while keeping her from the things she loved.

One day, when her bag was snatched by someone desperate to see what fascinating secrets it contained, she decided to flee. But fascinating people can never be invisible, even when they try to be, and soon she dragged across the country a tremendous train of the intensely fascinated. She constructed a decoy that looked fascinating enough from a distance to lure the attention of her following—and then snuck quickly away to the ocean.

Her head-start was slender, but it was enough to get her into an old green rowboat and far out to sea. But even away from land, the fascination of her was undiminished and she was pursued for many nautical miles by crowded pleasure crafts, people leaning perilously over the side, holding up their thumbs or making heart shapes with their fingers. She rowed for days, the sea and the fog drenching her excellent books and spoiling the fine food she'd brought with her.

Eventually, it seemed as if she'd finally escaped her following, and it had been many hours since the last person had sailed alongside to ask where she'd gotten her earrings. Exhausted, she put down the oars and let the little green boat drift with the tide. She slept.

When she woke up she found herself drifting towards a canoe that was being chased along the water by an armada of ladybird pedalos. The canoe passed close by and she got a good look at the woman in it. And, for the first time since she could remember, she was fascinated.

The woman in the canoe looked up at her and, before the most fascinating woman in the world could introduce herself, the canoe woman cried out for her to piss off and drown. How remarkable, she thought, to meet someone so fascinating all the way out here. And she smiled to herself as she pulled hard on an oar to turn her little green boat around, and row quickly after what surely was the most fascinating woman in the ocean.

The Reminder

Ida Keogh, winner, 2021 Shoreline of Infinity Magazine Flash Fiction Competition

"Don't forget to pick up the jackfruit," you say. Your voice is terse. I screw my eyes shut and hum a tune to drown out the sound. I did pick up the jackfruit. We sat here in the kitchenette, together. I cranked open the tin and you made steaming bao buns. I remember they became sticky in my mouth and had a slight tang of citrus underneath the hot satay sauce. You made a moaning sound as you sucked your fingers clean. Not for my benefit; you were still angry with me. But I did pick up the jackfruit. I did.

You weren't even here when you said it, you were shopping somewhere downtown. But it sounds like you're here in the room every time I go to open the fridge. It was our favourite spot to send messages. We'd both reach for a cold beer when we came home from a shift and hear each other's thoughts from the day. I open my eyes and see there's no beer left. I miss your reminders. All except this one. "Don't forget to pick up the jackfruit," you say again as I close the door.

At six o'clock I leave the flat and trudge through empty streets to get to the mini-market. Perhaps they will have jackfruit today, though I haven't seen any in months. Not that I could eat it now. After that night I'm sure it would only taste bitter.

When I get to the park the wind picks up and leaves whirl and eddy about my feet. Autumn already. There's a woman ahead of me on the path and I feel uneasy seeing another person. There are so few people around now, and the park can be dangerous after dusk. She's walking in a hurry, but when she gets to a particular bench she steers away from it, cutting a wide arc onto the grass before joining the path again. I know why. As I approach the bench myself I pause for a moment, clench and unclench my fists, then sit down. "To the woman with the Shih Tzu, you are so very beautiful. Meet me here at noon on Sunday?" The voice is gruff. I came here once, on a Sunday, with the romantic notion that some woman and her dog would turn up. But she never did.

There are three more messages on the way to the mini-market. I listen to each of them in turn. I wonder how long these ghost voices will persist. You thought it was strange when we couldn't delete the message you left for me. It was another small annoyance for you in a day full of them. A glitch in the system, you said. You would send a message to the controllers in the morning. But you never had the chance. You woke me up at dawn in a fevered sweat and they arrived too late to intubate you. "It's happening all over the city," they said. "Whatever you do, don't send any more messages." They needn't have worried. You were the only person I ever sent messages to, and we were hardly talking by then. That's what saved me.

  When I get to the mini-market Mr Khoury is there with an assortment of tomatoes, beans and courgettes from his allotment. I say hello and he gives me a watery smile but won't say a word. He's too scared to say anything, in case his speech ends up like those left over voices in the street. He has written what he wants in exchange for the food in crabbed handwriting I have to squint to read. It's mostly winter clothing. Even though they're a little wizened my mouth waters looking at real vegetables. I don't have anything he wants though, so I move on and rummage through prohibitively expensive canned goods before settling on a packet of out of date biscuits and a jar of home fermented sloe gin. There's a news stand near the exit, and I glance at the announcements on my way out. All messaging is still prohibited. The government is still searching for a vaccine. The usual.

When they brought in viral messaging it was revolutionary. No need for mobile phones any more. The smart virus could deliver your message directly to the brain of the person you wanted, provided they had the virus as well. Then location messages came in, and you could send your message to a precise coordinate to be picked up by the next person to go there. It was so cool. Celebrities left messages for fans outside venues. Poets left recitals on cliff edges. But like all novelties it passed into common usage and became banal. We weren't unique using the spot in front of the fridge for food reminders.

It was perfectly safe, they said. After extensive testing a few people developed sniffles, but nothing worse than the common cold. It was a smart virus, carefully created by geneticists and as easy to destroy as switching off your phone used to be, should you ever want to get rid of it. Nobody expected a variant would develop.

Our neighbour, Martha, lost her husband a few days after you were gone. He was abroad, somewhere in Thailand I think. With international communications at a peak it didn't take long for the variant to spread that far out. She hears him clear as a bell at her bedside, telling her, "I love you. Kiss the kids goodnight." Why couldn't I be left with comforting words like that?

I eat a biscuit and debate whether to go home or to visit the mass grave where you are buried. It's getting late, though, and I don't want to be out after dark with all those lost voices I might stumble on by accident. I head back to the flat. I look at the fridge and wonder if I should get some ice out. I drink the gin warm.

The Shop Game

Sam Payne, winner, Flash 500 Competition, Q2 2020

After the thing with the goldfish, the Joneses decide they need respite at Christmas. A little late notice, the social worker says, but it's not like you can blame them. Six families in the space of a year, the girl doesn't do herself any favours. But she's lucky, the Wilsons have agreed to take her in. They gave up fostering years ago but they're making an exception and the girl would do well to remember that. Mr Wilson used to be a train driver but now the only thing he rides is a mobility scooter. He sits on it in front of the television screen, cracking walnuts and almonds and tossing their half-crushed shells into an amber coloured ashtray.

    Each night, while the girl lies belly down on the rug colouring in pictures of cartoon families, he watches Only Fools and Horses and laughs himself into a coughing fit. When his face turns violet, Mrs Wilson rolls her eyes, puts down her crossword puzzle, and hefts herself up off her chair. She slaps him repeatedly on the back until he waves her away and the purple drains from his face.

The day before Christmas Eve, after a dinner of mashed potatoes and sausages and beans, they tell her they're all going out to play the shop game. At Christmas, the shopkeepers hide something in their window displays. Something odd or out of place. The game is to find it. It's easy at first. The tennis ball resting on a silver tray in the butchers, the small garden trowel in amongst the diamonds at the Jewellers, or the old violin, wood worn and missing a string, propped against a frying pan in the kitchen shop. But when they arrive at the haberdashery, they can't see anything wrong. The window display is filled with multi coloured wool bundles, patterned lace, and jars and jars of buttons and silver pins. The three of them are staring at all the beautiful things, but it looks perfect. Mr Wilson says, perhaps they're not taking part this year and Mrs Wilson says, come on, let's go.

But the girl won't leave. It starts raining, ice cold rain thickening to sludge. The kind of rain that wants to be snow but doesn't quite know how to hold itself together. Mr Wilson says he's had enough and steers his scooter up the street. The girl kicks at the wooden facade and pushes her palms against the glass. The rainy grey sludge fills the gutters and the gaps in the pavement. Mrs Wilson says, how about some hot chocolate? Come on, you'll catch your death standing there. But the girl doesn't move. She presses her forehead on to the glass and starts banging her brow against it. She's staring at the knitting needles, the crochet hooks, some red thread unravelling onto the white cloth but no matter how hard she looks, she simply can't find the one thing that doesn't belong.

The Wall

Mandy Wheeler, winner, Cranked Anvil Magazine Flash Competition, May 2022

The Man picks at the wallpaper. He wants to get underneath it, to bring the whole lot off in one.

"I thought you might like…"

A mug appears.

"Thank you," the Man says, still looking at the wall.

"Do you think you should..?" his son says. "I mean…the new people…"

"The new people are taking the wall down."

"But they might…"

The Man wonders when people had stopped speaking to him in complete sentences, and whether it happens to everyone.

In the surgery, the doctor glanced at the white spots on his arm.

"Perfectly natural… you know… when you are…"

"Old?" he suggested.

"You can roll your…"

He rolled his sleeve down. The white marks had increased recently, as though he was walking through a gentle but persistent snowstorm.

"It's just loss of pigment, nothing to…"

"Just?"

"Well, you know…"

Yes, he knew. Hair, teeth, sight, now pigment—all quietly leaving the party that had once been his life.

"Idiopathic Guttate Hypomelanosis," the doctor called it. "Guttate"—'resembling tear drops'."

"Ah well," said the Man. "At least Mother Nature has the decency to weep as she wrecks."

"If the wall's coming down, why…?"

He wants to say, "It's none of your business," but he's everybody's business nowadays, under constant surveillance for signs of eccentricity or worse.

"How's my favourite dad today?" the nurse will shout as she gurns in his face. "I'm fine," he'll want to say, "but I worry about you, if you think I'm your father."

He's got some purchase now. When a section splinters to reveal a fragment of brown and orange paper, he's back flicking through sample books with

Audrey, discussing the latest wipe clean wallcoverings, designed for the busy couple with a full life.

His son had reacted badly when the new owners said they'd remove the wall. "I was brought up in this house," he said. "And so was my father." The Man smiled apologetically and complimented the couple on their plans for an open plan lounge cum dining area. His son looked away. He wondered when his father had started ignoring him, and if it happened to everyone.

Finally, the paper is off.

"Do you remember these?" the Man says.

His son runs his finger up the ladder of horizontal lines drawn on the pitted plaster surface. He reads out the measurements, dates, his name. First Teddy, then Eddie. By 1975, he's Ted.

The Man waits until Edward notices the other line. He watches as he bends down, then reads a name the Man hasn't heard spoken aloud in years. Then a date, three years before Edward's birth.

Audrey had made sure Edward didn't see it, but now, at this late hour, the Man has stripped the wall bare in front of their son.

"What…?" Edward whispers.

His son is crouching down now, facing the wall. To protect them both, he stays there as his father starts to speak.

Things Left and Found by the Side of the Road

Jo Gatford, winner, Bath Flash Fiction Award, Feb 2018

Baby car seats, sometimes with babies in them, swiftly recovered. Nettles flourishing in the face of toilet breaks. Things said in anger and in tiredness, whipped free from wound down windows. Singular shoes. Houses turned into islands, refusing to bow to the bypass, clinging to their land. Roadkill; fox-ochre and badger-stripe and innards turned outer. And crows, wherever things are dead and forgotten. Shopping lists never fulfilled. Plastic bags, flocks of them, as everlasting as the old gods. GPS-related swearing. A horse, filthy white, the same colour as its hay, watching the traffic, dreaming of leaping three lanes to greener grass. Dozing lorry drivers, longwave sewn into their sleep. The shouts of children: *Cows! Red car! Lions! Lions? No. Cows!* The snap-shut replies of parents who should have stopped for a wee miles ago. Imaginary friends, abandoned because of older sisters who said they were babyish. Garden centres where time is liminal and space folds in on itself somewhere between the box shrubs and the trellis. Petrol stations, though never when you need one. Yawns no longer suppressible. A cigarette butt flicked through a window slot, its glowing ash streaking back inside to burrow into denim thighs. Traffic cones like shells for urban hermit crabs, crushed and dented, flashing silently into the night. A moment of lapsed concentration. A time when you wouldn't make it home for Christmas, or the weekend, or at all. A time when these were Roman roads and the unexpected turn would not have existed. A time when all of this was nothing but fields. Car parts, tyre skids, blood spots, and perfect cubes of safety glass. The knowing sighs of EMTs. Roadside recovery phones standing at respectful intervals like neon orange sentinels. Angels, fallen, bewildered in concrete, wondering where all the souls have gone.

Things The Fortune Teller Didn't Tell You When She Read Your Future

Iona Rule, winner, Retreat West Flash Competition, Dec 2021

that your secondary school boyfriend will snog your best friend at a *Coldplay* gig while you are in the toilet queue consoling a drunk stranger who has vomited in her handbag, that everyone else will know before you, that he'll tell you in a text the night before the Biology exam, where you'll sit at an uneven desk between the two of them and wonder if this is where you always were, that you will be become old friends with the stain on your bedroom ceiling in halls shaped like Australia, that you will stare at it as a drunk boy tries to heal your heart, or interprets your silences as consent, or when you wake beside a stranger and the night before is a dark hole of Jaeger bombs and you have never felt so alone, that when you meet him in the club having lost your friends his crinkled smile will make you stop searching, that his kindness will disarm you, that you will love him, in a way you will never love anyone else, that you will break his heart in a type of self destruction when your father dies in a car accident and you want the whole world to hurt too, that you will realise your mistake on graduation day, that you will tell him when he has already found someone else who looks so much like you that even you will need to look twice, that you will carry that what-if for as long as you live, that you will move from job to job until you start to move up rather than sideways, that you will swipe right on a whim and find your husband between the fuck boys, creeps and ghosts, that on your wedding night you will head to the shore and paddle in the waves sharing a bottle of champagne, look at the dead stars and feel small, that you will learn that a child is not as easy a thing to make as you always feared, that you will try and try and lose and lose until you have a daughter, that you'll wish she won't turn out like you and your wish will be granted, that the relationship you had envisaged will never happen, that there will always be a void between you neither of you can bridge, that your husband will die of a heart-attack the week before his 60th birthday, in the dairy aisle at Morrisons and the last words you say to him will be "Don't forget the toilet roll", that you will be choked by the things you never said but hope he knew, that you will cough crimson droplets onto the chipped porcelain at your granddaughter's dance recital, that you will return to the auditorium to your uncomfortable chair beside your silent daughter, that you will watch your granddaughter's bourrée that matches your frantic heartbeat, that you will clap and that you will keep clapping long after the lights go out.

To Pieces

*Abby Feden, winner, 2020 SmokeLong Quarterly
Flash Fiction Award*

The Sauders are almost prepared for winter. Silo shuttered, woodpile tarped, perennial bed snipped of spent blooms. Mrs. Sauder is canning in the kitchen, she leaves the radio loud to listen for bad weather. The girl is upstairs stitching. Mr. Sauder kills a pig in the barn.

Mr. Sauder slaughters to celebrate winter's first snow. He's past the hard part, bolt gun and leg binds, the thing is now meat and exsanguinates above a bucket in the barn. He walks the barnyard as it drips; he likes empty acres in the cold. Behind, the home looms. His daughter wilts in her room. His wife is an opaque haunt within the windows. Dead corn rattles. Lucky sows snuffle wet muck in their pen. Mr. Sauder's father taught him young to need such things more than anything else in the world.

The girl can barely stitch straight; she's crying her eyes gummy above a rip in her sweetheart's jacket. The shoulder and the sleeve have parted ways, sleeve cap gaping wide, fraying lips. His last name sweeps across the yoke like a long groan. Some lonely tune echoes up from the kitchen, her mother's whine adds to all this sad. She kicks up the pace of the pedal, shouts foul words when the thread gets caught.

Mrs. Sauder hears the sharp cut of a Singer going slack and sighs as her daughter spits. Her daughter never used language like that until her father spit it all right into her mouth. Just last week she'd seen a pale blue stain on the jugular of her daughter's throat and felt the ache that accompanies the loss of something loved. Out the kitchen window, Mr. Sauder paces the barnyard and she tries to remember the first time she thought she loved him. Green eyes smile up at her from the neck of a glass jar. Hulling soy is hard work. Behind her, the pressure canner whistles and she is comforted by bottles of beans kept still in water and salt. *I fall* the radio hums *to pieces.* Mrs. Sauder joins the verse.

The hard part of slaughtering a grower pig is knowing where to place the bolt gun. Despite his father's teachings, he cannot bring himself to use a blunt-bolt gun for fear the pig might wake as he is ripping through its jugular. The pointed-bolt feels good, the tinny click of a spring release and the crack of the skull are final sounds. Never mind the maybe of brain matter leaking to the ribs, the tongue, the feet—he'll put the meat in a trough. He puts a hand to his ribs. He'll rinse until it's all clean.

  Mrs. Sauder plunges her hands into un-hulled soybeans. Her daughter weeps in tune with the whistle of the pressure canner and she sighs. Some sweet-talking thing has eaten into her daughter's heart. She remembers everything and nothing from days spent just like that—the taste of lust memory only to her mouth. Never mind that now, she runs her fingers along the lids of canned beans and relishes the eternality of a tinny pop! New beans in the canner. Immortal ones on shelves. The whir of a Singer needle resumes. She feels the sudden urge to drown in salt water.

  Mr. Sauder slaughters a pig to celebrate winter's first snow because his father taught him this. As the grower pig exsanguinates above a bucket in the barn Mr. Sauder tends to lucky sows. He fills their trough and filters swill from their water. He cannot meet their eyes. As they nose their way through potato clippings and soy shells, metal rings in his mind. He wonders if they understand the sound of a pointed-bolt splitting up the skull.

The girl is crying so hard her stitches skew uneven through the sleeve cap. The shoulder yawns away in a loosening of thread. Downstairs her mother is popping the lids of canned beans and singing along wrong to some sad tune. She wasn't supposed to be wearing it but he liked the look of his name stitched down her back. Slam of a door like the blow of a bolt gun—this is not the first hurt she has known. A bit of blood would make the seam stick, she pushes her finger and the Singer eats.

It's starting to snow and Mr. Sauder is eviscerating a pig. He's ticked the list, penetrating bolt-gun, bucket for blood, corpse bath, bristle shave, inedible organs on the floor. His father taught him how to skin a pig quick but this ordeal drags in an unusual way. Mrs. Sauder pickles grower pig feet and nibbles them down in the spring. His daughter chokes against the taste. Quick swipe of a folding knife and the pig is missing his chest. Mr. Sauder has it in his hand. He feels sick and slides the bones back into the pig. Mr. Sauder considers swallowing the bolt gun. The pig is whole again.

In the kitchen Mrs. Sauder cranks the radio to drown her daughter's upstairs ache. *I fall to pieces* she sings and realizes the song has changed. Same tune, sadder story, it's not her favorite but it will do against the silence of the house. It's snowing outside. Cold glass goes for a soak in hot water; she is appreciating the way the bottle prepares itself to entomb green eyes when one shatters in the sink. Someone is singing *pieces each time* and she guts her thumb on a sneaky shard lost within suds. Pressure canner whistles, the girl upstairs screams, the barnyard sounds like cracked bone. The sink is full of blood. She can't bear it. The lids won't pop.

From the barn a bolt-gun blows, blood drips tinny in a bucket. The sleeve gapes as the girl cries, cradling all her hurt. The radio sings and Mrs. Sauder hums the wrong tune. Pressure canner steams. Something breaks—glass, bone, baby. The prairie is swallowed by snow.

Treating the Stains and Strains of Marriage
Sherry Morris, winner, Retreat West Flash Fiction Competition 2019

She's in the supermarket—the laundry aisle to be precise. Today's special offer: colour catchers. "Aha," she says.

Reaching high, on tip-toe, using a mop from the next aisle, she knocks two rows of bright-orange boxes into her cart. Watches as twenty, thirty, maybe fifty postcard-size cartons tumble down. She races for the checkout, nearly running over an old lady. There's no guilt—old ladies are past their sell-by date. She still has shelf life.

In her kitchen, she tapes small white squares together into one large sheet with a fervour that would make an evangelical nod and shout "Amen!" The cat pokes its nose in, smells danger, backs out. As she works, her lips recite the product's promises like a prayer.

Effective at all temperatures.
Prevents greying.
Prevents residual dirt redepositing.

At *Prevents run accidents*, she pauses. He'll need one too. Double-strength knowing him.

Inspired, she grabs Mr Muscle for an added bit of sparkle. It's not cheating. Potential double-coupon bonus: shapely calves, a toned stomach, banished bat wings. She reads the label. *Causes serious eye irritation.* She shrugs. Most husbands do. Further on it says *Avoid prolonged skin contact*, but that's what she craves. This can't hurt any more than anything else in their marriage. She applies liberally. Her skin prickles. She doesn't know if product or anticipation makes her feel like a pincushion. She's glad a slow spin cycle is recommended. She'll hold on tight.

They're meeting at 3pm today.

She won't think about when, exactly, the heavy purples and greys sneaked under the door where the cracks were too wide. How some days black pooled on the ceiling, oozed down the walls, saturating her so completely she couldn't even slide out of bed.

She went crusty, rusty, musty. He asked what was wrong, but words and feelings clogged her heart. Not even a bottle of Drano had helped.

He went slimy and grimy, walking in gutters, slipping down drains, disappearing for weeks at a time. She no longer wanted his dirty hands on her. He moved out and dark blues swallowed her whole.

But the cat demanded to be fed, that she get out of bed. This and long soaks in fabric conditioner were the start. She marvelled at the crud that slid down the plughole.

"A vow is not just for now," he'd said. They'd both been so light, so bright back then.

She rang him while holding a bottle of Febreze. Suggested they meet in Soft Furnishings. Now cocooned within her sheet, she waits for it to work. The cat arrives to check on her.

"Colour catchers have a money-back guarantee," she says. "That's not what I want back."

The cat yawns—stares at her with clear glass-green eyes, begins his own methodical wash. She admires his agility, his self-care ability, the mix of colours in his calico coat. She remembers the rainbow she'd seen that morning. How its faint arc brightened the dark sky.

Twenty-One Species of Fish Called Sardine
Rosaleen Lynch, winner, Oxford Flash Fiction Prize, Summer 2021

Mam wants a mermaid instead of me and though I slip out of her like a fish in the birthing pool on a rainy day, I have no tail or scales, and I do not smell of the sea, and when Pa tries to give her this squalling too-many-limbed me, she tells him "Some cactuses don't grow towards the light," but she doesn't mind when I'm swaddled and even though she's not got baby shoes or any clothes with legs, she does not go out to buy them and keeps me zipped up like a clam in sleeping-bag suits or wraps me in layers of long seaweed coloured shifts and smocks she ties with twine, and tells me "Scales are like if cactus spines were flat, or umbrellas closed when there's no rain," and she does not encourage me to walk, so I sit with her as she tells me of her dream of Pa and her dancing on the boardwalk at Coney Island and she sings, "Somewhere beyond the sea..." or I lie on my back or belly to slide across the floor, legs lost in the folds that follow, or I ride on Pa's old skateboard with the scull and crossbones, a knot to stop hems getting caught, and I sail out the back door and down the garden path, like a minnow on a stream, and she calls me Guppy, Betta, or Angelfish and when she's angry Sprat, and when the time comes for me to start nursery she puts it off, saying she doesn't want to be left like a lone cactus on a dessert shore, me gone in the morning, Pa gone to security work at night and asleep in the day, until he comes to say goodbye to me out back, and stands in sunlight at the garden fence, hand over one eye to see, turning it into a telescope, to say "I spy a mermaid swimming in the bluebell sea," a bottle hanging from his other hand, uisce beatha, the water of life, company on the boat at night, that harbours the pirate radio-station, that Mam listens to, out of reach of the Gardai, the guardians of the peace, and when Pa's gone Mam goes on the phone, requesting songs, laughing like she's never done with Pa and waves from the bedroom window, the mermaid tail cactus he gave her on the sill and she looks past the field I'm in and down the hill to the sea, and the wind picks up, the net curtains fill like sail, and the air carries words of hers, like "freedom", "escape" and "yes" and the wind vane turns and the white net curtain with it, to slap across Mam's body and shroud her face, a ghost now standing in the window, as if all that's left of her is the mermaid tail, and as I watch, I feel the bluebell sap stick my toes together, and I lie back in the grass and by my face in the bluebell sky hangs the first moon daisy which I pick and pluck the petals from to confirm I should spend that summer, weaving a mermaids tail from dried seaweed, seagrass, long grass and weeds to hide in the shed, to show Mam when we come home, from her first day of work and mine of school, where I spend the hours kicking off my shoes, the teacher complaining about spills and falls and other children copying me, until the floor is littered with shoes and he tells me to pick up every one and return them, and I do, to the fish tank that has lost its fish and watch the shoes swim, laces flailing in the bubbles coming from the fake plastic treasure chest, and Mam has to come from the canning factory to pick me up, smelling of sardines and oil, and says, "There are twenty-one species of fish called sardine," and asks why can't I be one, as she lifts me up from the chair I was told to wait on, wrapping my duffle coat round my bare legs and feet, as she takes me to the car, and says, "The sea urchin cactus only wakes at sunset," and straps me in the front passenger seat and we drive, I can't see where, but it's not home, and the radio plays "This is the sea" by the Waterboys and I fall asleep and wake in quiet until Mam's car door opens to let in the sound of the seagulls and sea and closes, and I slip out of the seat belt and up on my knees to lean on the warm dashboard, and watch through the windscreen, what she calls cactus clouds with little pricks of rain, roll in, as she disappears as if she was never there, into the sea, the rain making the glass between us a blur, and I switch on the radio, the orange light of the dial like a little sunset in the dark of the car and I remember the sea urchin cactus Mam said only woke at sunset as I listen to the presenter announce a special request, from The Last Pirate to his treasures at home and "What shall we do with the drunken sailor" plays and dovetails into the traditional Irish song, "Óró 'Sé do bheatha 'bhaile", O row, you are welcome home, making my neck prickle, and still leaning on the now cold dashboard, the skin on my arms goose-pimples and my legs go numb, as I wait for Mam to come out of the sea.

Undergrowth
Melissa Bowers, winner, 2021 SmokeLong Grand Micro Contest

He is three years old and thinks the word for plant is *planet*. I should correct him, but I don't, because I suspect it won't last—the same way *brefkast* and *sank you* sprouted from his mouth for months and then somehow blossomed properly, even without adequate sunlight. Every time we pass the farmland on that stretch beyond Highway 101, he watches as the tractors overturn the dirt, rolls his window down to smell the tillage. They're getting ready for new planets, he says, breathing deeply, filling his lungs with the scent of soil.

He is nine and learning about space in school: how our galaxy alone is 100,000 light-years across, and how a single light-year equals nearly six trillion miles, and how there are two trillion galaxies, and out of all those planets how can we believe ours is the only one that matters? I tell him he is not as small as he feels. His doctor tells me she is not seeing enough progress. We're hoping for visible growth, she says. Brighter spots, happier episodes. I imagine him the way he looked when he was born: shriveled but strong, coated with proof of his own germination. Solid, at least. Something more than a shadow.

He is twelve and I find him in the redwoods just before dusk, kneeling in the brush under the trees. With his hands he clears away thick clumps of vegetation—methodically at first, then frantic, the greenery piling up behind him like a hillside. What remains is an emptiness. What remains is a bare patch on the world, as if he has ripped a swath of hair out of the forest. It's going to be a garden, he says, I'm growing this, see? But I don't. I can only see what is gone.

He is seventeen and one night he doesn't come home. I call his friends, his love, our neighbors. I drive the edges of the farmland and shout his name through the wind and park at the mouth of the woods because he has to be here somewhere, trapped just below the surface. With both palms, I press against the ground and wait to feel it give. Instead it swells upward from the roots, it bulges in spots, orblike. Beneath the earth there is the unmistakable hum of something spinning and spinning and spinning.

We Will Go On Ahead and Wait for You
Michael Logan, winner, 2008 Fish One-Page Fiction Prize

Fukuko and her daughters huddle together upon the bluff, far above the churning river. A wintry gust of wind lifts Kaiya's best kimono, exposing her spindly young calves. *She has grown so fast*, Fukuko thinks. *I'll need to let it out soon.* Then she remembers it no longer matters, and her legs wobble beneath her.

I have no choice, she tells herself. Hajime has already been rejected twice, but he will volunteer again. Yet there is no hope as long as he remains a husband and father. And although he never openly blames her or the girls, when he looks at them now his eyes are bitter studs in a wax mask. Each further rejection, each one of his students that flies in his place, will only harden the eyes, once so warm. Better a short separation and honourable reunion than a life filled with such looks.

Fukuko's legs find their strength again.

"Why are we here?" asks Kaiya.

"We are here for your father," Fukuko replies.

"Father come now?" asks Chieko.

"Not yet. We must go on ahead and wait for him."

Kaiya sniffles and Chieko, forever copying her elder sister, joins in. Fukuko pulls their small bodies closer, plants a kiss on each forehead, and steps over the edge. The girls scream and struggle against Fukuko's embrace, but her grip remains firm as they accelerate downward.

Fukuko closes her eyes and pictures Hajime in the cockpit of a fighter plane; the screams transform into the whine of his straining engines. Bullet-holes bloom on the windshield, but they cannot stop the god wind. Hajime's eyes are as warm as the rising sun on his headscarf and an easy smile curls his lips as he dives, coming to join his family.

While My Wife is Out of Town

Jude Brewer, winner, 2017 Retreat West Flash Fiction Competition

Two light bulbs burned out in the basement, so I used the flashlight app on my smartphone while carrying my cat with the other hand to ward off any ghosts.

I'm brushing my teeth in the shower while shampooing my hair and lathering my chest hair and the places on my back I can't quite reach, because I can't just stand in front of the mirror brushing my teeth doing nothing.

The four-dollar cinema is playing a documentary on cats in Turkey tonight, and I'm enamored with their relationships, the cats and the people and how they depend upon each other, the cats for the food and the people for the soft company, but I'm also reminding myself that in three weeks the credit card bills are due and so is rent, and the car payment is due in three days, and I'm eating two delicious pizza slices.

I'm pretty sure everyone has been having ads broadcast to them in their sleep since everyone is drinking La Croix these days, and this is by no means an endorsement, just an observation.

I'm not feeling well so I'll hide like a house cat where no one notices, somewhere they can't ever find me, somewhere I can't hear the cellphone buzzing.

The dishes in the sink are getting crusty so I'll let them soak in room temperature water for five days while my wife is out of town.

The fresh smelling laundry is still warm and piled up on her side of the bed so I'll play the big spoon.

The piano won't play itself, and my hand stabs the keys to see if a song can write itself, and the silence twanging off her guitars is louder than the empty fridge humming.

The pizza delivery guy just wants his tip, not an invite to hang out and play catch up on all these years we never shared; that's cool, maybe next time, next pizza.

The classics on my shelf could use a nice crease in their bindings so I tuck myself into this cooling laundry pile and feel my eyelids lower over blurring prose I've longed to live within.

These sneakers are cursing under my barking arches, and the autumn air rings with leaf blowers, and a chirrup follows my jog before, in one grand leap, I'm now chasing it.

On stage, a sixty-two-year-old-woman sings, her body contorting along with a prerecorded track designed by an underground 70s band none of us have ever heard, and her voice wavers how the open mic host paces with his eyes darting around the room, like he can't decide if she should get a second song like everyone else has so far.

The bar's macaroni and cheese takeout tastes fine in the dark, in my quiet home, my cellphone buzzing, the screen's light filling my eyes, her message saying, "How was your day?"

Contributor Biographies

Kathryn Aldridge-Morris's flash narratives have been published in many literary journals and anthologies, including New Flash Fiction Review, Pithead Chapel, Bending Genres, Janus Literary, and Ellipsis Zine. She is the winner of the 2022 QuietManDave Prize for flash fiction and the 2022 flash fiction contest organised by Welsh publisher Lucent Dreaming. She was a finalist in Flash Frog's Blue Frog Award and New Flash Fiction Review's annual Flash Fiction contest. She has been shortlisted and highly commended in the Bath Flash Fiction Award, and for the Aesthetica Creative Writing Award, and her work has been nominated for the Pushcart Prize and Best Microfiction.

Gail Anderson's short fiction, poetry and life-writing have taken first prize in competitions including the Scottish Arts Trust Story Award, The Edinburgh Award for Flash Fiction, Reflex Fiction (2019 and 2022), the Writers' Bureau, Winchester Writers' Weekend and the Winchester Writers' Festival, and she has been shortlisted five times for the Bridport Prize. Recent work is published in The Southampton Review, Mslexia, Popshot, Ambit, Epiphany and elsewhere. She lives in Scotland and sails a little boat in the Firth of Clyde.

Jack Barker-Clark is a British fiction writer. His stories have featured widely in the UK, including in 3:AM Magazine, Litro, New Critique and the Prototype 4 anthology. In the US, his poems and prose are published in Diagram, Hobart, Ninth Letter and elsewhere.

Zoe Barkham has loved books and writing for as long as she can remember. She has produced stories and biographical pieces, poems and educational texts, and especially relishes the challenges of making one word do the work of six in flash fiction. She lives in London with her husband and their enormous dog, where she enjoys renovating dolls houses, walking the said enormous dog, gardening and persuading herself that anything bought at an auction is a bargain. She is currently working on her first novel and dares to hope that this time she might actually finish it.

Laurie Bolger is a London based writer and founder of The Creative Writing Breakfast Club. Laurie's work has featured at Glastonbury, TATE, RA & Sky Arts. Laurie's writing has appeared in The Poetry Review, The London Magazine, Moth, Crannog, Stand, & Trinity College Icarus. This year Laurie's writing was shortlisted for The Bridport Prize, Moth Poetry Prize, Live Canon, Winchester & Sylvia Plath Prizes. Laurie is currently working on her first full length collection *Lady*. www.lauriebolger.com @lauriebolger

Andrew Boulton is a lecturer in creative advertising and creative writing at the University of Lincoln. He is the author of a bestselling book on copywriting and a children's book called *Adele Writes an Ad*. His stories have been published in journals and competitions including the Bridport Prize, Retreat West, Lunate Fiction, Tiny Molecules, Spelk, Reflex, Bath Flash Fiction anthology, Cranked Anvil and Storgy. He lives in Nottingham with his wife, daughter and a chubby cat.

Melissa Bowers is a writer from the Midwest of the USA. She is the winner of the SmokeLong Quarterly Grand Micro Contest, the 2020 Breakwater Review Fiction Prize, the 2020 F(r)iction flash fiction competition, and The Writer's inaugural personal essay contest. Her work was selected for the 2021 Wigleaf Top 50 as well as The Best Small Fictions 2022, and has also appeared or is forthcoming in The Cincinnati Review, The Greensboro Review, New Ohio Review, River Teeth, The Forge, and The Boston Globe Magazine, among others. www.melissabowers.com @MelissaBowers_

Sharon Boyle lives in East Lothian, Scotland, and writes around her family and part-time job. She has had several short stories and flash pieces published on-line and in magazines, including Ellipsis Zine, Retreat West, Reflex Fiction and Cranked Anvil. Currently, she is writing a YA novel mystery/thriller she hopes will be a firecracker success. She tweets as @SharonBoyle50 and has a luddite-basic blog at https://boyleblethers.wordpress.com Her dream is to have a writing shed so she can potter and procrastinate in total peace.

Creator of STORYBOUND and Storytellers Telling Stories, **Jude Brewer** works daily as a writer, showrunner, voice actor, and sound designer. Between producing for Pulitzer-Prize-winning and breakout artists, his work has been featured on every major podcast platform, receiving praise from KCRW, Radiotopia, PRX, Lifehacker, Vulture, the AV Club, the NYTimes, Bello Collective, Discover Pods, and Retreat West UK. He lives in Portland, Oregon.

Peter Burns is a writer from Glasgow, where he also works as a Registered Nurse. He has previously been published in the Bath Short Story Anthology 2021, the National Flash Fiction Day Anthology 2022, Flashback Fiction, FlashFlood Journal and Janus Literary Journal. He was placed first in the Flash 500 competition in autumn 2020, and second in summer 2022. He holds an MA in Creative Writing and a BA in Literature with honours, both from the Open University.

Claire Carroll lives in Somerset, UK, and writes experimental fiction about the intersection of nature, technology, and desire. She is also an AHRC-funded PhD researcher at Bath Spa and Exeter Universities, where she explores how experimental writing—particularly short stories and prose-poetry—can reimagine how humans relate to the natural and non-human world. Claire's short stories and poetry have been published by journals including Gutter Magazine, perverse, Lunate Journal, The Oxonian Review, and Short Fiction Journal, shortlisted for The White Review's Short Story Prize, and the recipient of the Essex University and Short Fiction Journal Wild Writing Prize.

Whenever possible, **Matthew Castle** reads and writes speculative fiction, and science or history-tinged narrative nonfiction. Most of the rest of the time he's either working in medical publishing, or chasing after/being chased by his two young children. His work has appeared in Shoreline of Infinity, Kinfolk magazine, and the Damn Interesting website. www.mattcastle.co.uk

Kim Catanzarite is the author of the award-winning *Jovian Duology*, a sci-fi thriller. She is a freelance writer and editor for publishers and independent authors, and she teaches copyediting for Writer's Digest University. Her Self-Publishing 101 blog discusses the ins and outs of indie life as well as all things writing craft (www.authorkimcatanzarite.com). She lives on the east coast of the USA with her husband and daughter.

Kevin Cheeseman is a retired biochemist who lives in Buckinghamshire with his wife, Annie. Having spent half his career in academia and the other half in drug development for a pharmaceutical company, he feels liberated now that he's allowed just to make stuff up. He writes flash fiction and short stories, and his pieces have won or been placed in competitions run by

Writing Magazine, Writers' Forum, 1000 Word Challenge and Wild Atlantic Writing Awards, amongst others.

Originally from Manchester, **Tim Craig** lives in Hackney in east London. Winner of the Bridport Prize for Flash Fiction in 2018, his short-short stories have been placed or commended four times in the Bath Flash Fiction Award and have appeared in the Best Microfiction 2019 and 2022 anthologies, as well as many literary journals in both the UK and USA. His debut collection, *Now You See Him*, is available from Ad Hoc Fiction.

Kit de Waal's debut novel *My Name Is Leon* won the 2017 Kerry Group Irish Novel of the Year Award and was adapted for television by the BBC. Her second novel, *The Trick to Time*, was longlisted for the Women's Prize. She is also the author of a young adult novel and a collection of short stories, and editor of the anthology of working-class memoir, *Common People*. A Fellow of the Royal Society of Literature and Professor and Writer in Residence at Leicester University, her memoir, *Without Warning and Only Sometimes*, was published in Aug 2022.

Emily Devane is a writer, editor and teacher from Ilkley, West Yorkshire. Her short fiction has been widely published, most recently in Ambit, Janus Literary, Smokelong Quarterly and Best Microfiction Anthology. 'The Hand That Wields the Priest' won the Bath Flash Fiction Award and was a Best Small Fictions finalist. Emily has also won a Northern

Writers' Award and a Word Factory Apprenticeship. She was shortlisted for the 2022 Mogford Prize and was awarded second place in the Bath Short Story Award. Emily teaches creative writing, co-hosts Word Factory's Strike! Short Story Club and is a founding editor at FlashBack Fiction.

Monica Dickson (she/her) is a short fiction writer from Leeds. Her work has appeared in Splonk, jmww, Anti-Heroin Chic, X-R-A-Y and elsewhere. She has been longlisted for the Reflex Flash Fiction competition and the Bath Flash Fiction award, shortlisted for the TSS Flash 400 competition and won the 2019 Northern Short Story Festival Flash Fiction Slam with 'One of the Girls', originally published by Dear Damsels. Another story, 'Receipts', published by Spelk, was subsequently selected for the inaugural Best of British and Irish Flash Fiction list (BIFFY50). Monica is a 2021 graduate of the Northern Short Story Festival Academy.

Dara Yen Elerath's debut collection, *Dark Braid* (BkMk Press), won the 2019 John Ciardi Prize for Poetry and was longlisted for the Julie Suk award. A Best of the Net, Best Small Fictions and Pushcart Prize nominee, she is the recipient of the Bath Flash Fiction Award and the New Flash Fiction Review Award. Her work has appeared in journals such as The American Poetry Review, AGNI, Poet Lore, Plume, Boulevard, Sixth Finch, Tahoma Literary Review and elsewhere. She received her MFA in poetry from the Institute of American Indian Arts and lives in Albuquerque, New Mexico.

Abby Feden is a fiction writer living in Stillwater, Oklahoma. She is the winner of the 2020 SmokeLong Quarterly Award for Flash Fiction. Her work has been nominated for The Best of the Net, a Pushcart Prize, and appears in Smokelong Quarterly and Best Small Fictions 2021. Feden received her MFA from Western Washington University and is in her third year of Oklahoma State University's PhD in Creative Writing.

Jeremy Galgut lives in Nottingham, England. He works as a computer programmer, but prefers to write fiction. He has had over forty stories published in a range of magazines and anthologies and has won first prizes in the Writers & Artists, Short Fiction Journal, New Writer and Brittle Star competitions. Publications his work has appeared in also include the Bridport Prize Anthology, The Edinburgh Review and the Middlesex University Press Anthology. Examples of his published work can be found on the 'Short Fiction' page at www.jeremygalgut.com.

Frances Gapper lives in the UK's Black Country. 'Plum Jam' (FlashBack Fiction), 'She's Gone' (Wigleaf) and 'For a Widow' (Twin Pies) were published in Best Microfiction 2019/21/22, and 'Harry' won Silver Apples Magazine's Flash Cat contest 2022. 'Lawn' (a longer story) placed second in the 2021 SaveAs Writers fiction prize, sponsored by the University of Kent; judge Amy Sackville said: "I loved the fabular weirdness of this, the queer erotics of it, the strange and familiar world of it, and the unexpected turns that it took; and most particularly, the distinctive and peculiar narrative voice."

Jo Gatford writes flash disguised as poetry, poetry diguised as flash, and sometimes things that are even longer than a page. Her chapbook, *The Woman's Part*, was published by Stanchion Books in January 2023 and her short fiction and poetry have appeared most recently in The Lumiere Review, Full House Lit, Voidspace and The Woolf. She was once left on her parents' driveway in a baby car seat (but apparently only for a minute).

Rosie Garland has a passion for language nurtured by public libraries. She writes long and short fiction, poetry and sings with post-punk band The March Violets. Latest collection *What Girls do the Dark* (Nine Arches Press) was shortlisted for the Polari Prize 2021. Her novel *The Night Brother* (Borough Press) was described by The Times as "a delight...with shades of Angela Carter." Val McDermid has named her one of the most compelling LGBT+ writers in the UK today. She has been blessed by The Sisters of Perpetual Indulgence. www.rosiegarland.com

Vanessa Gebbie writes for the joy of it and the challenge. She's a novelist, poet, short form writer, teacher and editor. She's won a few things, including prizes for flash, short story, poetry and travel writing. Her work has been translated into Portuguese (novel) Punjabi (poem) Greek (story) Russian (essay) Italian (flashes) Vietnamese (flashes) and German (novella in flash). Her current project is a compilation of writing games, illustrated with example responses from her students (Ad Hoc Books 2023), and forthcoming is a 4-month stint as inaugural Writer-in-Residence for Petersfield Museum and the Edward Thomas Archive. www.vanessagebbie.com

Lucy Goldring calls herself a Northerner despite living in Bristol all her adult life. She began writing fiction aged forty, only twenty years after she said she would. Lucy has a story in Best Microfiction 2022. She's been shortlisted by the National Flash Fiction Day three times and twice selected for their anthology. In her past life, Lucy worked in the voluntary sector, promoting sustainable solutions. When not writing or kid wrangling, she binges on sitcoms and worries about climate change. @livingallover livingallover.com

Tania Hershman is the author of three collections of short stories and flash fiction, four books of poetry, a hybrid novel and a hybrid book inspired by particle physics. She lives in Manchester, UK, is the founder of the ShortStops online short story hub and has a PhD in Creative Writing inspired by physics. www.taniahershman.com @taniahershman

Sarah Hilary's debut, *Someone Else's Skin*, won the Theakstons Crime Novel of the Year and was a World Book Night selection. The Observer's Book of the Month ("superbly disturbing") and a Richard & Judy Book Club pick, it was a

Silver Falchion and Macavity Award finalist in the US. Her first standalone, *Fragile*, was published in 2021. Mick Herron called it "a dark river of a book", while Erin Kelly said, "Timeless, tense and tender, Fragile will worm its way deep into your heart." Her new book, *Black Thorn*, will be published in 2023. www.sarahhilary.com

Sara Hills is the author of the award-winning flash collection *The Evolution of Birds*. Her stories have been selected for Wigleaf's Top 50, Best Small Fictions, and the BIFFY50, as well as widely published in anthologies and magazines, such as SmokeLong Quarterly, Cheap Pop, X-R-A-Y, Fractured Lit, Cease Cows, Flash Frog, and Reckon Review. Originally from the Sonoran Desert, Sara lives in Warwickshire, UK. @sarahillswrites

Marissa Hoffmann's stories have won the Mslexia Flash Fiction Prize, the Bath Flash Fiction Award, the Bath Short Story Award and the Fractured Lit Anthology Prize. They've also been a finalist at CRAFT Flash Fiction, short listed at the Bridport Flash Fiction Prize, long listed for the Mogford Short Story Prize, and they appear on the Wigleaf 50 longlist and Best of British and Irish Flash Fiction (BIFFY) list. Her work has received nominations for the Pushcart Prize, Best Small Fictions and Best Micro Fiction. She's an Associate Editor at Atticus Review, and working on a short story collection. www.marissahoffmann.com @hoffmannwriter

Patrick Holloway is a writer of stories and poems. He is the 2021 winner of the Molly Keane Creative Writing Competition, the Allingham Flash Fiction Competition, and the Flash 500 competition. His work has been published by The Stinging Fly, Overland, The Irish Times, Poetry Ireland Review, The Moth, Southword, among others. His story, 'Laughing and Turning Away' won 2nd place in the Raymond Carver Short Story Contest. He has been shortlisted for numerous other prizes including: Bath Short Story Prize, Moth Poetry Prize, Moth Short Story Prize, and the Alpine Fellowship for Fiction. He is editor of The Four Faced Liar.

Mary-Jane Holmes has won the Bath Novella-in-Flash Prize, Dromineer, Reflex Fiction and the Mslexia Flash prizes. She has been shortlisted for the Beverley International Prize and won the Bridport poetry Prize. Her novella-in-flash, *Don't Tell the Bees*, is published by Ad Hoc Fiction. Her flash Fiction collection *Set a Crow to Catch a Crow* was published by V Press in 2021. Her work appears in publications including Mslexia, The Lonely Crowd, Prole, The Journal of Compressed Creative Arts, Tishman Review, Barren, Spelk, Cabinet of Heed, Firewords, Flashback Fiction, Fictive Dream, Phare and anthologies including Best Small Fictions 2014/16/18/20 and Best Microfictions 2020.

Barbara Kuessner Hughes was born in Malaysia, grew up there and in Singapore, and now lives in England with her husband, two daughters and two dogs. She has won or been listed in flash fiction and short story competitions such as Reflex, Flash 500 and Cranked Anvil, and had stories published by Storgy, East Of The Web, Quarterly Literary Review Singapore and other publications. This autumn she is due to have work appear in Amarillo Bay journal. www.barbarakuessnerhughes.com

Vicki Jarrett is a novelist and short story writer from Edinburgh. Her first novel, *Nothing is Heavy*, was shortlisted for the Saltire Society Scottish First Book of the Year 2013. Her collection of short stories, *The Way Out*, published in 2015, was longlisted for the Frank O'Connor International Short Story Award, and shortlisted for the Jerwood Fiction Uncovered Prize and the Edge Hill Short Story Prize. Her latest novel, *Always North*, came out at the end of 2019 from Unsung Stories and was shortlisted for the Red Tentacle (Novel) Award in the Kitschies 2019.

Gaynor Jones is the recipient of a 2020 Northern Writer's Award from New Writing North for her short story collection, *Girls Who Get Taken*. She has won first prize in several short fiction competitions, including the Bath Flash Fiction Prize and the Mairtín Crawford Short Story Award, and has placed or been listed in others including the Bridport Prize and Aesthetica. She is working on her first novel and is represented by Laura Williams at Greene & Heaton. www.jonzeywriter.com

Louise J Jones writes fiction and poetry and makes colourful things from yarn and thread. She was born in Manchester, is half-Welsh, but has lived most of her life in and around London so she feels she is a Londoner more than anything else. She loves going to art galleries and bookshops— especially mooching in their cafes. She has an MA in Creative Writing and has had her writing published in several anthologies. She won the Fish Flash Fiction Prize in 2019. She lives in Hertfordshire and has one very wonderful daughter.

As the daughter of an antiquarian book dealer, **Taria Karillion** grew up surrounded by far more books than is probably healthy for one person. Having spent her childhood in a castle cottage, her genre preference started out as fantasy, but grew to encompass science fiction after an accident with a staircase, a copy of *The Hitchhikers Guide to the Galaxy* and a nasty attack of gravity. A Literature degree, a journalism course and some gratuitous vocabulary overuse later, her stories have appeared in a Hagrid-sized handful of anthologies and have somehow won enough literary prizes to fill his other hand. Despite this, she has no need as yet for larger millinery.

Ida Keogh is a sci-fi writer living in Surrey. She won the British Science Fiction Award for Shorter Fiction in 2020 and the British Fantasy Award for Short Fiction in 2021 for 'Infinite Tea in the Demara Café', NewCon Press. She has been shortlisted for the Writing the Future Short Story Prize. Her debut novella, *Fish!,* is out now with NewCon Press. @silkyida

Brenden Layte (he/him) is an editor of educational materials, a linguist, and a writer. Recesses won The Forge Literary Magazine's 2021 Flash Fiction Competition. Brenden's work has also appeared in places like Entropy, Lost Balloon, Pithead Chapel, and Ellipsis Zine. He lives in Jamaica Plain, Massachusetts with his girlfriend and cat. @b_layted

Cathy Lennon lives in Lancashire and writes short fiction. Her work has appeared in print and online, in places such as Arachne Press, Journal of Compressed Arts, NFFD, Reflex and others.

D. Brody Lipton studied creative writing and education at Sarah Lawrence College and Boston University. His stories have appeared in places such as SmokeLong Quarterly, Spelk, Literary Mama, and Cowboy Jamboree. He teaches in Houston, Texas.

Michael Logan is Scottish writer based in Rome. His fiction is as unfocused as he is, ranging from opening fleeting windows into a character's life to creating fantastical and often silly worlds. The story in this anthology, at under 300 words, is the hardest thing he has ever had to write (it took three hours to decide to change one word, then two to decide to change it back again). Michael is the author of four novels, including the Terry Pratchett Prize winner, *Apocalypse Cow*.

Rosaleen Lynch is an Irish youth and community worker and writer in the East End of London with words in lovely places

including New Flash Fiction Review, HAD, Fractured Lit, Craft, SmokeLong Quarterly, Jellyfish Review, EllipsisZine, Mslexia, Litro and Fish, shortlisted by Bath and the Bridport Prize, a winner of the HISSAC Flash Fiction Competition and the Oxford Flash Fiction Prize. @quotes_52
52Quotes.blogspot.com

Fiona McKay lives beside the sea in Dublin, Ireland, with her husband and daughter. She is a flash fiction writer and is also revising a novel. Writes with Writers' HQ. Her novella-in-flash longlisted in the 2022 Bath and Reflex Novella competitions. Words in various places, including: Reflex Fiction, Janus Literary, Scrawl Place, EllipsisZine, The Waxed Lemon, The Birdseed, Twin Pies, Bath Flash, Lumiere Review, Books Ireland. Nominated for Best Microfiction 2021. Supported by Arts Council Ireland Agility Award. @fionaemckayryan

Pauline Masurel is a gardener who lives in South Gloucestershire. Her short and tiny fictions have been included in anthologies, published online, broadcast on radio and performed at events in Bath, Bristol, Gloucestershire and beyond. www.unfurling.net

Originally from Missouri, **Sherry Morris** (@Uksherka) writes prize-winning fiction from a farm in the Scottish Highlands where she pets cows, watches clouds and dabbles in photography. She reads for the wonderfully wacky Taco Bell

Quarterly and her first published story was about her Peace Corps experience in 1990s Ukraine. www.uksherka.com

Rachel O'Cleary grew up in Wisconsin, but now lives with her husband and three children in Ireland, squeezing her obsession for flash fiction into the spaces between school runs with the help of Writers' HQ. Recent and forthcoming publications include Smokelong Quarterly, The Forge, Fractured Lit, Milk Candy Review, and Wrongdoing Mag. @RachelOCleary1

Valerie O'Riordan's work has appeared in Tin House, LitMag, the Manchester Review and other journals. In 2019, she won an O. Henry Prize. She is Senior Editor at The Forge Literary Magazine and teaches creative writing at the University of Bolton, England.

Gillian O'Shaughnessy is a journalist and a short fiction author who lives by the ocean in Fremantle, Western Australia. She worked for the Australian Broadcasting Corporation as a radio broadcaster and news reporter for 25 years and now spends her time interviewing authors and writing flash fiction. gillianoshaughnessy.com @GillOshaughness

Phil Olsen is a writer from Liverpool with a Creative Writing MA from the University of Manchester's Centre for New Writing. His short fiction has been published by Ad Hoc Fiction, Cōnfingō, The Liminal Residency, Storgy and Strix, and has been commissioned for 'Journey Through Objects with Bedwyr Williams' (Science Museum, 2021-22) and 'Weekend of Words' (Victoria Baths, 2019). Prizes include University of Liverpool Short Story Competition 2022, Northern Short Story Festival 2017 flash slam and Writing on the Wall's WoWFest 2016. Phil is Fiction Editor at Sabotage Reviews and Contributing Editor at Vestal Review. polsen.co.uk @Liverpolsen

Sam Payne holds a BA with first class honours in English Literature and an MA (Distinction) in Creative Writing. She is currently Fiction and CNF Editor at Janus Literary and her flash has placed in several competitions including Flash500, Retreat West and the Bath Flash Fiction Awards. She's been published in Fictive Dream, Flashback Fiction, 100-word story and Popshot Quarterly. @skpaynewriting

Doug Ramspeck is the author of nine collections of poetry, one collection of short stories, and a novella. Individual stories have appeared in The Southern Review, The Georgia Review, Iowa Review, and elsewhere. His short story 'Balloon' was listed as a Distinguished Story for 2018 in The Best American Short Stories. A retired professor from The Ohio State University, he lives in Black Mountain, North Carolina, USA. dougramspeck.com

Angela Readman's stories have won the New Flash Fiction Review Competition, the Costa Short Story Award, and the Mslexia Story Prize. Her debut collection *Don't Try This at*

Home won The Rubery Book Award and was short listed in The Edge Hill Prize. *The Girls are Pretty Crocodiles*, her second story collection, was published in 2022. She lives in Northumberland and also writes poetry. Her new poetry collection *Bunny Girls* (2022) is with Nine Arches.

Electra Rhodes is an archaeologist, who lives in Hertfordshire. Her poetry and prose work is widely published across a range of formats. Recent pieces appear in the Parthian Press anthology, *An Open Door: New Travel Writing for a Precarious Century*, and in the Fly on The Wall Press anthology, *Demos Rising,* (both 2022). She's one of The London Library's Emerging Writers for 2022/23, and is working on an intersectional biography of the British landscape.

Jane Roberts's fiction features in a variety of publications and presses including: *100 Stories for Haiti, 100 Voices for 100 Years* (Unbound), Aberystwyth University, Arachne Press, Flash: The International Short-Short Story Magazine, Litro, NFFD Anthologies, Refugees Welcome, Retreat West, Seventy2One, *Stories for Homes*, The Emma Press, The Lonely Crowd, The Mechanics' Institute Review, The Shadow Booth, Under The Radar (Nine Arches Press), Unthank Books, Wales Arts Review, Visual Verse, and Valley Press's *High Spirits: A Round of Drinking Stories* (Best Anthology, Saboteur Awards 2019; The Publishers Association 2019 Summer Recess Reading list for Parliamentarians). www.janeehroberts.wordpress.com @JaneEHRoberts

Iain Rowan is the author of the novel *One of Us* and has had over forty short stories published. Iain came second in the 2020 Costa Short Story award, won a Northern Writers Award, and in the past has been shortlisted for the Bath Novel Award and the Crime Writers' Association Debut Dagger. He's represented by Tom Drake-Lee at DHH Literary Agency. iainrowan.com @iainrowan

Nicholas Ruddock is a Canadian physician and writer, twice a winner at Bridport, shortlisted as well for the Sunday London Times Short Story Award, the Moth Poetry Prize, the Manchester Metropolitan Short Story Award. His most recent novel, *Last Hummingbird West of Chile*, is set primarily in Dorset, Singapore, and London. NicholasRuddock.com

Iona Rule lives in the Scottish Highlands and once went on a date that involved getting her fortune read via tarot cards. She can't remember any of the predictions. She came second in the Bath Flash Fiction Award and was included in a recent Fractured Lit anthology. Her writing can be found in Atlas and Alice, Janus Literary and Perhappened.

Helen Rye's stories have won the Bath Flash Award, the Reflex Fiction Prize, and been placed/nominated/shortlisted/published in many other fine places. She has an MA in Creative Writing from UEA, where she was the Annabel Abbs scholar. She is a senior editor at SmokeLong Quarterly.

Bean Sawyer is a writer, a stained-glass artist/illustrator and part- time teaching assistant at a Steiner Waldorf school in Pembrokeshire, West Wales. She's currently querying her first novel *The Lost Song*, a YA fantasy adventure told through prose and poetry, and was longlisted for the 2021 and 2022 Bath Children's novel award. She also won the Writers & Artists Killer Fiction competition and last year had a short story recorded for the Alternative Stories Midwinter Monologue podcast. Bean regularly takes part in the Globe Soup challenges and won the 2021 September micro-flash competition. www.beansawyer.co.uk

Seamus Scanlon is a working class writer from Galway who examines the ambiguity of the Irish towards violence. His Fish flash fiction winner, 'The Long Wet Grass', based on The Disappeared in Northern Ireland, found resonance with many people. Drama versions followed with performances in New York, Galway (home audience—always a tough one!), Hastings (UK) and the Japanese language version in Tokyo (www.mcgowantrilogy.com). Recent achievements include 'Beauty Curse' in the 2022 Fish Anthology, 'Waiting for the Sea' in *Cry of the Poor* (Culture Matters, 2021) and 'On the House' in *From the Plough to the Stars* (Culture Matters, 2020). www.seamusscanlon.com

Bernadette M Smyth is a short story and flash fiction writer from County Louth, Ireland. Her stories have been short-listed for various competitions including the Fish Short Story

Prize, the Bridport Prize, and the Bryan Mc Mahon Award. Her work has also been broadcast on RTE Radio 1 as part of the Francis Mac Manus Short Story Season. 'In the Car' won the Fish One Page Prize in 2009.

Brianna Snow writes small stories and lives in big cities.

David Swann's novella, *Season of Bright Sorrow* (Ad Hoc Press), won first prize in the Bath Novella-in-Flash Award. In 2022, his novella, *The Twisted Wheel*, finished runner-up in the same contest, and will be published soon. Dave's story, 'Drought', won the 2016 Bridport Flash Fiction Competition, his eighth success in a Prize that he judged in 2013. His other publications include *The Privilege of Rain* (based on his experiences as a writer-in-residence in jail, and shortlisted for the Ted Hughes Prize). A former local newspaper reporter, and a toilet cleaner in a legendary Amsterdam night-club, he teaches at the University of Chichester, and makes fires on his allotment.

Dri Chiu Tattersfield (they/he) writes speculative short fiction, games and zines. Inspired by moss, they are interested in exploring the interfaces between worlds, particularly the past and the future and science and poetry. He is from Taipei, Taiwan, and currently teaches high school physics.

Sharon Telfer has also won the Bath Flash Fiction Award (twice) and the Reflex Fiction Prize. Her stories have been selected for Best Small Fictions, Best Microfictions, National

Flash Fiction Day anthologies, and the BIFFY50 lists. Her debut flash fiction collection, *The Map Waits*, is published by Reflex Press and was longlisted for the 2022 Edge Hill Short Story Prize. She's a founding editor at FlashBack Fiction, the online zine showcasing historical flash. She lives in East Yorkshire, not quite close enough to the sea. @sharontelfer

Elisabeth Ingram Wallace is the winner of the Mogford Short Story Prize, the Kaleidoscope Writing the Future prize, and a Scottish Book Trust New Writers Award. Her stories have been published in SmokeLong Quarterly, Wigleaf, Barrelhouse, and many anthologies, including Best Microfiction 2021. Her flash has won competitions at The Forge Literary Magazine, Fractured Lit, TSS, and the QuietManDave prize at Manchester Metropolitan University. Most recently, her 1000 word story 'Opsnizing Dad' was made into an opera, performed at the University of St Andrews. She is working on a collection and a novel. elisabethingramwallace.com

Rob Walton is from Scunthorpe, and now lives in Whitley Bay. His flash fictions, poems and short stories for adults and children have appeared in various anthologies and magazines in the UK, USA, Canada, Ireland and New Zealand. Arachne Press published his debut poetry collection, *This Poem Here*, in March 2021. Other publishers include Flash Frontier, Paper Swans, the Emma Press, Bloomsbury, Smith/Doorstop, Dunlin Press, Dostoyevsky Wannabe, Popshot and Strix. @robwaltonwriter

Terry Warren b. 1961 Silver End. He studied Fine Art in Braintree and London. Lives in a small hamlet near Bridport, West Dorset where he continues to draw, paint, and write. He currently works as Head of Marketing for a national construction company and as an Access Consultant. 'Buttercups' was his first published work.

Rowena Warwick is a writer and poet based in Oxfordshire, UK. She has an undergraduate diploma and an MA in creative writing, both with distinction. She has been placed or listed in competitions for poetry, flash fiction, short story, memoir and the novel. Her writing can be seen in numerous publications. She is currently recovering from a career in the health service. @rowena_warwick

Mandy Wheeler is a writer and creative practice tutor who used to be a radio director and producer. She's written comedy scripts for the BBC and won a Bitterpill Theatre scriptwriting award. Her short stories have picked up awards from the Cranked Anvil Press, Flash 500, and the Women on Writing short fiction contest. She's been shortlisted for the Bridport Prize and Fish Short Story Award and won the 2022 Scottish Arts Club Short Story Award.

Joanna Will lives in Italy where she is writing a novella and a weekly piece of flash fiction. She also spends her time learning Italian, teaching creative writing and attempting to train her chickens to perform simple tricks. She has written three screenplays that were filmed in Mozambique and has written a book about Lyme Regis. Most of her stories are born while drinking her indispensable 6am pot of tea.

Jo Withers writes short fiction for open minds. She is a previous winner of Molotov Cocktail Flash Monster, SmokeLong Quarterly's Comedy Award, Furious Fiction, Reflex Press Flash Fiction Competition Winter 2021 and The Caterpillar Story for Children Prize. @JoWithers2018

Alison Woodhouse is a writer, creative writing tutor and mentor and helps run the Bath Short Story Award. Her short fiction has won a number of competitions and many other pieces have been placed or shortlisted. Her novella in flash, *The House on the Corner*, was published by AdHoc Fiction in 2020 and her flash collection, *Family Frames*, in 2021 by V Press. @AJWoodhouse

Competition Descriptions with Story Titles

Bath Flash Fiction Award hosts two international flash fiction writing competitions; the Bath Flash Fiction Award, and the Bath Novella-in-Flash Award. The Flash Fiction Award has a 300-word limit and there are three rounds per year: March to June, July to October, and November to February. In addition to winning cash prizes, entrants have the opportunity to appear in our print and digital anthology collections, and also as single author novellas-in-flash. Our books are published by the award-winning small press Ad Hoc Fiction, and are available to buy from their own independent bookshop as well as worldwide from Amazon. www.bathflashfictionaward.com
Cleft by Gaynor Jones • 24
Snow Crow by Doug Ramspeck • 130
The Button Wife by Dara Yen Elerath • 142
The Hand That Wields the Priest by Emily Devane • 154
Things Left And Found by the Side of the Road by Jo Gatford • 181

The Blue Frog is Flash Frog's annual flash fiction prize. Each year the contest features a different theme based on what type of stories they wish they'd seen more of in the queue. The Blue Frog also has a different Guest Judge each year and awards a total of $700 in prize money as well as signed books and original art. flash-frog.com/contest
Press 3 for Random Track by Dri Chiu Tattersfield • 101

No-one should have to choose between food or fuel. Thanks to Tania for making this book happen. The **Bridport Prize**

Flash Fiction Prize alumni includes Kit de Waal who won twice, returned as a judge and recently mentored our black writer residency. We run a bursary scheme for free entries to our international writing competition with no proof of income required. We want to discover new writers in Flash Fiction as well as Memoir, Novel, Short Story and Poetry. We are open to anyone writing in English from anywhere in the world. Now more than ever, words matter.
www.bridportprize.org.uk
Buttercups by Terry Warren • 22
Drought by David Swann • 33
Mum Died by Rowena Warwick • 89
Polio by Nicholas Ruddock • 99
Sins of the Heart by Kit de Waal • 128
The Grand Finale by Tim Craig • 152

The **Bristol Short Story Prize** is an annual international competition based in Bristol, UK which is now in its 15th year. The competition is open to all writers and accepts submissions on any theme or subject and although there is a maximum word count, there is no minimum, and flash fictions often make it into the longlist and beyond. BSSP publishes an anthology every year which contains the top three prize winning stories plus the 17 other stories which were selected for the competition's shortlist.
www.bristolprize.co.uk
Mum's the Word by Valerie O'Riordan • 91

Cranked Anvil was established in 2012 and, since 2019, has been publishing short stories and flash fiction online and in

print anthologies. They run various writing competitions; their flash fiction competition runs quarterly, and is open for submissions all year round. They also provide resources, exercises and advice for writers. www.crankedanvil.co.uk
Glass by Fiona McKay • 48
The Most Fascinating Woman in the World by Andrew Boulton • 166
The Wall by Mandy Wheeler • 177

The **Edinburgh Award for Flash Fiction** is an annual £2,000 prize for writers worldwide and stories on any topic up to 250 words, run by the Scottish Arts Trust, alongside the Scottish Arts Club Short Story Competition. www.scottishartstrust.org/flash-fiction
The Letter from the Home Office by Gail Anderson • 159

The **Federation of Scottish Writers flash fiction competition** runs annually as part of a wider competition (there are five categories: open poetry, open short story, flash fiction, Scots and Scottish Gaelic) and the current word limit for flash fiction entries is 500 words. www.federationofwriters.scot/competition
Self/Less by Electra Rhodes • 120

The **Fish Flash Fiction Prize** is probably one of the shorter flash prizes, with its 300 word maximum. Originally the idea was to fit each flash on one page, and we called it the Fish One-Page Prize. They are quick (if not always easy) to read, and to be SO surprised, taken aback, shaken-up and entertained by so many of them made it all fun. And the Fish Anthology benefited from having them alongside the stories that could drift up to 5,000 words. I love all the forms in which we receive flashes, the joke, the twist, the mystery, the hanging cliff, the poem, and the rest of them. I love it when you get to the end and the meaning slowly washes over you and you have to read it again to confirm that yes, all of that was hidden in the text and like a truffle had just enough showing or smelling so that you got it subliminally. Magic! www.fishpublishing.com/competition/flash-fiction-contest

Both On and Off by Jack Barker-Clark • 20
Darling Mummy by Zoe Barkham • 29
Fall River, August 1892 by Sarah Hilary (Fish Criminally Short Histories) • 38
In the Car by Bernadette M. Smyth • 69
Morning Routine by Kim Catanzarite • 85
Teavarran by Louise J Jones • 135
The Long Wet Grass by Seamus Scanlon • 164
We Will Go On Ahead and Wait for You by Michael Logan • 200

Flash 500 started life in 2010 as a quarterly competition purely for writers of flash fiction. We believed then (and still do) that, because of how hard it is to encompass a complete story in so few words, flash fiction is one of the hardest forms in which to achieve success. Over the years the site has grown and now includes annual short story and novel categories. www.flash500.com

15-C-47662 by Patrick Holloway • 1
Coffee by Barbara Kuessner Hughes • 26
Last, Best Hope in a Shade of Orange by Taria Karillion • 77

Sometimes there's Compassion in a Punch by Peter Burns • 132
The Shop Game by Sam Payne • 174

FlashBack Fiction is an online journal dedicated to historical flash fiction, prose poetry and hybrid work. We decided to start this project after multiple conversations about where to find great historical flash fiction, and where to submit our own work. Our aim is to collect and celebrate shortform work — both traditional and experimental — that in some way engages with the historical. What 'historical' means we're leaving up to our writers and readers; we look forward to the conversation. Flashback Fiction runs occasional competitions for themed flash fiction. flashbackfiction.com
Bedlam by Jo Withers • 17
Plum Jam by Frances Gapper • 98

Flashbang was a flash fiction contest masterminded by Sarah Hilary to promote CrimeFest (an annual crime fiction convention held in Bristol). Contestants had to tell a compelling crime story in no more than 150 words. It ran from 2012 to 2017. flashbangcontest.wordpress.com
Search History by Iain Rowan • 118

The **Flash Fiction Festival** celebrates the short-short-story worldwide, with both an in-person festival held annually in July and regular online festival days. Several flash fiction competitions are run during the festival. www.flashfictionfestival.com
Lessons in Attachment Parenting by Sara Hills • 81

The **Forge Literary Magazine** is a passionate group of diverse, international writers. We share editorial duties, pay our contributors, and our tastes are wide-ranging and eclectic. We don't believe money should be a barrier to access, so our flash contest (and our magazine) offers free submissions. Literary excellence is our only criteria. We believe in prompt responses, even for contests. We open on September 1st and publish the winning fiction and nonfiction pieces in November. The staff works together on an initial read, adding favourites to a longlist. Our editors reread and create a shortlist which goes back to our hardworking readers, who vote again. We're a non-profit organisation, are all volunteers, and we love what we do. forgelitmag.com
Recesses by Brenden Layte • 106
Scrolling Facebook Memes Waiting for the Paediatrician by Elisabeth Ingram Wallace • 111

Globe Soup run a variety of flash fiction competitions throughout the year. Some contests are designed to test particular writing skills and techniques, some feature unusual or challenging prompts, while others are completely open and a great way for writers to put their best short fiction forward in the hopes of winning a cash prize and seeing their story published on the Globe Soup website. www.globesoup.net
Lost Appetite by Bean Sawyer • 84

The **Gloucestershire Writers' Network** was founded in the 1990's by Roger Drury and Jamila Gavin, author of award-winning children's novel, Coram Boy. The GWN ran

workshops and readings, produced newsletters and collections of writers' work, Gloucestershire Writes, which were loaned through the library service. The GWN's competition event at the Cheltenham Literature Festival has been a principal feature of the GWN's work. Many local writers have benefited from the links created by the GWN and from winning the competition—which has poetry and prose categories—in developing their careers. gloswriters.org.uk
I Found Myself Lost by Pauline Masurel • 62

Hysteria is the annual women's writing competition, originally run by the Hysterectomy Association (which closed in 2019). It features three categories: short stories, poetry and flash fiction, with differing word limits each year. 2023 will be the competition's tenth year. hysteriawc.co.uk
Sea Change by Sharon Telfer • 116

Gary Kaill and Hannah Clark founded **Lunate** while studying for their MA in Creative Writing at Manchester Writing School in 2019. They aimed to provide a new journal for writers who shared their taste for smart, well structured, creatively ambitious literature. Although Lunate no longer publishes Flash Fiction, the Lunate500 competition was a fabulous opportunity to celebrate the diversity of the genre with a series of talented judges who each helped shape the competition and made it something very special. www.lunate.co.uk
The Eight Year Hope of Us (as seen on TV) by Lucy Goldring • **148**
The First Man on The Moon by Rosie Garland • **150**

Mslexia is an award-winning magazine supported by Arts Council England. Its mission is to help women express themselves and get their writing noticed: in print, online and in performance. Mslexia was granted charitable status in 2019 in recognition of its work to fulfil this mission. Flash fiction was added as a new category to Mslexia's annual writing competitions in 2016. www.mslexia.co.uk
After the Armourers by Marissa Hoffmann • 13
Blue Hills Yonder by Joanna Will • 18

The first **National Flash Fiction Day** in the UK took place in 2012. Founded by Calum Kerr to promote flash fiction worldwide, it has taken place annually since then and is now directed by Ingrid Jendrzejewski and Diane Simmons. As part of the celebrations, the first Micro Fiction Competition in 2012 asked for unthemed flash fictions of 100 words or fewer and received hundreds of entries. The competition continues to thrive and receives entries from around the globe. It now awards cash prizes for First, Second and Third places, as well as seven Highly Commended. You can read all the winners since its inception on our website: nationalflashfictionday.co.uk
Fifth Grade by Brianna Snow • 43
Fly by Rob Walton • 44
For You, I Am by Alison Woodhouse • 47
Never Let Me Go by Cathy Lennon • 93

The **New Flash Fiction Review** was founded in 2014 by Meg Pokrass as a journal dedicated to the love of short but powerful writing. While the journal has fiction in the title, it's never been

too concerned with the lines between fiction and non-fiction, and in 2020 the journal added the Micro Life feature where CNF is included with Flash Fiction. NFFR has published stories in a variety of ways including special features or themes dedicated to topics like: Triptychs, Horoscopes, Holiday Noir, Love Stories, and others. In 2018, the journal hosted its first contest, at that time named the Anton Chekhov Prize. In 2021, the contest was renamed to the New Flash Fiction Prize. The contest offers the fun of having a guest editor, getting to celebrate writing in ways beyond publication, reading anonymously (which the editors enjoyed so much they added it to regular submissions as well) and the contest helps support journal expenses. The prize issues have included some of NFFR's most memorable work.
newflashfiction.com

Ten Months with Octopus by Angela Readman • 137

The award-winning **Northern Short Story Festival** (NSSF) is the North's only festival dedicated to celebrating and championing the short story. "NoShoSto" started in 2016, and was the brainchild of then Festival Director SJ Bradley. We aim to bring the best in short story writing to Leeds, to celebrate the many brilliant writers already in the region, and support the excellent independent presses which do great work nationwide. Our motto is "affordable, accessible, representative, locally run." We are part of the Leeds Big Bookend and are funded by arts@leeds (2018-22) at Leeds City Council. Our Academy scheme is further supported by the Walter Swan Trust. We've had 3 Flash Fiction slams since 2016. They are always brilliant fun and bring out the

competitive and performance spirit in the writers who take part. The audience love it too as they get to cheer on their favourite writers! bigbookend.co.uk/nssf
One of the Girls by Monica Dickson • **94**
The Haunted Pan by Phil Olsen • **156**

The **Oxford Flash Fiction Prize** is a new international competition with a mission to discover The Greats in flash fiction from all around the world. It inspires and develops writing talent by providing motivation, opportunity for all, and international recognition. Oxford has inspired some of the greatest creative writers and poets in the world, and we're here to expand its legacy into flash fiction. Founded in Oxford in 2021 as a Community Interest Company, the Oxford Flash Fiction Prize is dedicated to encouraging new voices from all backgrounds by finding new approaches to how competitions are run. We are committed to proactively tackling social inequalities and barriers, celebrating flash fiction, and encouraging new voices. Competitions have the power to inspire, encourage, and elevate writers wherever they are on their journey. oxfordflashfictionprize.com
Twenty-One Species of Fish Called Sardine by Rosaleen Lynch • **194**

The **QuietManDave Prize** celebrates short-form writing and the life of someone who loved to experience new places, art and events and write about them. The Prize was established in memory of Dave Murray, who entertained and informed many through his quietmandave blog, and is organised by Manchester Metropolitan University's Writing and Theatre

schools. Dave embraced writing relatively late in life but did so with a passion, and the Prize seeks to enable and promote new writing, offering awards and runner-up prizes for Flash Fiction and Flash Non-Fiction. The QuietManDave Prize has been supported through the generosity of family and friends of Dave. www.mmu.ac.uk/qmdprize
Double Lives by Kathryn Aldridge-Morris • 31
Granny Smith, Queene by Elisabeth Ingram Wallace • 53

The **Reflex Fiction Flash Fiction Competition** was a quarterly international flash fiction competition for stories between 180 and 360 words run by independent publisher, Reflex Press, until 2022. www.reflexfiction.com
A Girl's Guide to Fly Fishing by Mary-Jane Holmes • 11
Fly Away Home by Helen Rye • 45
Good For Her by D. Brody Lipton • 51
Mouse by Gillian O'Shaughnessy • 87

Retreat West has been running flash fiction competitions for 10 years. In that time, it has published hundreds of stories online and in the anthologies from the annual Retreat West Prize. It also hosts weekly flash writing sessions, Friday Flashing, on Zoom; provides online and email flash fiction courses; and generally loves all things flash fiction! retreatwest.co.uk
Emmylou, Patron Saint of Dirt-Poor Folks by Sharon Boyle • 35
Things the Fortune Teller Didn't Tell You When She Read Your Future by Iona Rule • 183
Treating The Strains and Stains of Marriage by Sherry Morris • 191
While My Wife is Out of Town by Jude Brewer • 202

Shoreline of Infinity is based in Edinburgh, Scotland and we publish an award winning science fiction magazine, featuring stories, poems, art and non-fiction. It's a print and digital publication, released 4 times a year, and we have readers and contributors from all over the world. Every summer we announce a flash fiction competition for our readers, and the top three stories are published in the winter issue, and the winning story is read by a professional actor at a live and online event. The competition is themed - this year's was: my Pet. Next year's? Wait and see! www.shorelineofinfinity.com
A Choice for the Golden Age by Matthew Castle • **5**
La Loba by Vicki Jarrett • **72**
The Reminder by Ida Keogh • **169**

Small Wonder Festival is a festival dedicated to short-form writing. Held annually at Charleston in East Sussex, the festival often holds a flash fiction slam. www.charleston.org.uk/festival/small-wonder-festival-2022
The Lighthouse Project by Vanessa Gebbie • **161**

SmokeLong Quarterly was established in 2003 by Dave Clapper. Past editors-in-chief have been Randall Brown and Tara Laskowski. The current editor-in-chief is Christopher Allen. We are dedicated to bringing the best flash narratives to the web quarterly, whether written by widely published authors or those new to the craft. The term "smoke-long" comes anecdotally from the Chinese, who noted that reading a piece of flash takes about the same length of time as smoking a cigarette. *SmokeLong Quarterly* does not condone smoking, but

we do enthusiastically condone reading flash when you have a few minutes. SmokeLong runs a two biennial competitions: the SmokeLong Quarterly Award for Flash Fiction (The Smokey) for stories up to 1000 words, and SmokeLong's Grand Micro Contest (The Mikey), for microfiction up to 400 words. www.smokelong.com
To Pieces by Abby Feden • 186
Undergrowth by Melissa Bowers • 198

The **Strands International Flash Fiction Competition** is a competition for stories between 300 and 1000 words that is run six times a year by Strands, an independent group of artists and writers from across the world. strandspublishers.weebly.com/strands-international-flash-fiction-competition.html
If a Tree Falls by Rachel O'Cleary • 66

WritersandArtists.co.uk is the go-to resource for writers and illustrators. As the online extension of the Writers' & Artists' Yearbook, you can register for free and gain access to hundreds of expert advice articles and inspirational author interviews, a lively online community, events and editorial services for every stage of your creative journey. We offer varied writing competitions that are free to enter and we have a yearly bursary scheme and encourage all writers to apply for an event or editing service. We've ran successful flash fiction contests and our annual short story competition and the Working-Class Writers' Prize are yearly staples.
Battle Hymn of the American Republic by Jeremy Galgut • 15
Silent Space by Jane Roberts • 126

Each month, **Writers Forum magazine** helps thousands of new and aspiring writers achieve their dreams. It's packed with up-to-date market information, advice from experts in the publishing industry and inspiring stories and tips from fellow authors and writers. We also feature interactive reader workshops in fiction and poetry so you can see at first hand how to improve and successfully target your own writing.Our monthly writing contests for fiction, poems and flash writing are world-famous, awarding cash and prizes each issue, plus publication in the magazine. The flash fiction competition has a different theme each month. writers-forum.com/flash-competition
The Cinders of 2021 by Kevin Cheeseman • 144

Writers' HQ has been helping writers finish their stories since 2012. What started as two friends making time and space to write has grown into the most word-slinging, tea-drinking, story-writing, biscuit-dunking, procrastination-busting, support-giving writing community around, with thousands of writers getting their words onto paper and into the world. The Writers' HQ Flash Quarterly Competition and From LGBTQ+ WIth Love Contest published over 30 beautiful pieces of flash fiction from around the world. WHQ is also the home of Flash Face Off - a weekly flash fiction incubator that has produced hundreds of published and prize-winning stories from the Writers' HQ community. writershq.co.uk
Fever by Claire Carroll • 40
Groceries by Tania Hershman • 56
How Much Rain Can a Cloud Hold? by Laurie Bolger • 59

Index of First Lines

1. Your teeth are smudged blueberry. **1**

1996. The night before you go, we choke on our wine watching Jarvis Cocker waft farts at Wacko Jacko. **148**

Aoccdrnig to rscheearch at Cmabrigde Uinervtisy it deosn't mttaer in waht oredr the ltteers in a word are... **111**

And the days were made of auguries. **130**

After the thing with the goldfish, the Joneses decide they need respite at Christmas. **174**

Baby car seats, sometimes with babies in them, swiftly recovered. **181**

Dad tells Mom to feed the damn cat. **51**

Darling mummy, Well, the big day is here at last! **29**

"Don't forget to pick up the jackfruit," you say. **169**

Even by his own high standards, The Great Fantoni's world tour had been a triumph. **152**

Even when severed from the body the limbs of an octopus can function on their own. **136**

For you, I am **47**

First it was cartons and tins on the worktops, then newspapers on the stairs. **93**

For what Giorgi did, the clansmen could have thrown wood tar on him, rolled him in feathers, hanged him. **13**

Fluorescent men in high-vis vests hang like fruit in the trees. **53**

From our ladders we can see the plum-blue Malverns. **98**

Fukuko and her daughters huddle together upon the bluff, far above the churning river. **200**

Grandma ate poison five times before it killed her. **87**

He is three years old and thinks the word for plant is *planet*. **198**

Her **66**

Here in the dark you could be any age. **40**

His parents argue. **126**

I cull through your belongings for a recent photo and find everything but. **81**

I see Gwen at the school gates and she does this thing where she's looking but not seeing... **31**

I opened a can of cat food and grabbed a saucer and one of the forks nobody likes... **85**

I sit rigid, body taut as wooden chair. **17**

I want you to make me pregnant. **56**

Ignition—3, 2, 1. **45**

I'm rushing to push my lunch box in to my bag when I see these two who must be flying a kite on the green triangle... **44**

In 1953 the polio virus hovered over the summertime streets of Toronto, it multiplied in the warmth... **99**

In hills north of the famous resort, we slip stiles beyond the dam, looking for signs. **33**

internet dating **118**

Is hard to bind heart to harrow and drill. **18**

I steered through fantastic streets of boisterous traffic, past glittering buildings, and footpaths that moved with shoppers. **69**

It is 3:00AM and 告白氣球 by Jay Chou comes on the karaoke machine. **101**

It spins up on a thermal, fluttering in a sparrow-brown envelope
(second class) and when she reaches to catch it, her hot-air balloon lurches. **159**

It starts with a single word. **120**

It wasn't the fly fisher's fault she got caught up in his line… **11**

It was such a very hot day, the air flapping like a thick cloth in her face. **38**

Julia Ward Howe in her room on the second floor of the Willard Hotel gathers the sheets around her. **15**

Mam wants a mermaid instead of me and though I slip out of her like a fish in the birthing pool on a rainy day, I have no tail… **194**

Margaret drinks coffee rarely; it's too emotive. **26**

Max watched the boy through the telescope for over an hour. **161**

Mum died reaching for a packet on the top shelf of a kitchen cupboard. **89**

My heart sank. **116**

Noun, a fissure or split **24**

On the phone to your daughter all winter. **20**

People come. **22**

Push it down. **48**

Scene: *The Royal Ball.* **144**

She can never believe how bright the gorse is, laid in great yellow arcs across the land. **135**

She needs bread. **128**

"So, have you had any paranormal experiences in this house?" **156**

She's in the supermarket – the laundry aisle to be precise. **191**

She wants to be the girl in the passenger seat, feet up on the dashboard, playing with the radio while he drives. **59**

She watched as he tucked into the grub. **84**

That evening, the fish left a strange taste in my mouth. **154**

that your secondary school boyfriend will snog your best friend at a *Coldplay* gig while you are in the toilet queue… **183**

The bank sits a half mile out, as if it doesn't want anything to do with the rock-bottom town it serves. **35**

The boys call her Wardy, like she's one of the lads, a bit of a laugh. **94**

The button wife bends her body across the bed, but the cloth husband is not interested in touching her. **142**

The Captain wakes, reborn into the *Golden Age* for the sixteenth time. **5**

The Man picks at the wallpaper. **177**

The resonance of tires against the wet road is a mantra, strong and steady. **164**

The Sauders are almost prepared for winter. **186**

The year it happened was the year that I moved into my own head. **62**

Three times with his grunting and the calloused hand over my mouth: first, the kitchen wall rough at my back... **91**

To: Audit Officer 5688A **77**

Two light bulbs burned out in the basement, so I used the flashlight app on my smartphone while carrying my cat... **202**

Upon landing, Johannes Kepler looks back at Earth, a blue-green ball tossed high in lunar sky. **150**

We learn that there are tubes inside of us with sleeping babies. **43**

We thought we'd be safer away from the city. **72**

When Da booked our first holiday, a weekend in a caravan in St. Andrews, Ma wept. **132**

When it became clear she truly was the most fascinating woman in the world, everybody wanted to be near her. **166**

You're eight or nine and you can barely fit in the pantry because it's mostly taken up by a broken washer... **106**

Acknowledgements

It takes a village to create a book, especially when the book's editor has never done anything like this before. This one began to become a reality after a conversation with Abi Hynes—thank you, Abi, for your encouragement, I'm not sure I would have moved forward without it, and for your proofreading. Thanks also to Marie Leadbetter, who donated the cover image of the gloriously-coloured fuel pump, and to Katie Jacobs, who designed the amazing cover—while she was in the middle of moving countries.

This book would be entirely blank were it not for, firstly, the organisers of all the competitions featured: thank you to all those of you who put forward your first-prize-winning stories, contacted the authors for permission, and for your general enthusiasm and encouragement. Secondly, the most enormous thank you to all the authors, for generously donating stories for no fee and no free contributor copy, to allow us to raise as much as possible for fuel poverty charities. Particular thanks to Nicholas Ruddock, who proofread the entire book, and Gail Anderson, whose invaluable layout advice has made this look far more professional than it would have otherwise.

The richness and diversity of the flash fictions here is, I believe, quite astonishing and rarely found anywhere. My initial mission of exploding the myth of a formula for winning stories has been well and truly fulfilled. I wanted to leave you with a further reading suggestion: I came across short short stories in the late 1990s, just as I was beginning to write, and I wanted to take a moment to thank Robert Shapard and James Thomas, the editors of those Sudden Fiction and Flash Fiction anthologies that lit the flash fiction spark in me. They are still producing new anthologies collecting together the most wonderful writers of the shortest of stories, so when you've finished this book, do go and get hold of one of theirs.

Finally, I can't know as I write this what might happen in the UK in terms of fuel prices, the existence of "warm banks" for people who can't afford to heat their homes, and the need, so urgent at this time, for charities dedicated to helping those in what we now call "fuel poverty". Enormous thanks to all these charities, and I hope that our small contribution helps in some way.